The Edinburgh Anthologi

Volume Two

Heartsick

and other stories

Edited by
Sara Cameron McBean
and Claire Rocha

Scottish Arts Trust

Scottish Arts Trust

The Scottish Art Trust was founded in 2014 and has established itself as an innovative and forward-looking charity. The Trust has created a series of nationally and internationally significant arts events, helping to promote the work and livelihoods of more than a thousand artists, writers and musicians.

Most of this work has been achieved through the work of volunteers. Their hard work has paid off and is generating increasing attention from creatives, audiences and press, as well as potential donors and partner organisations.

The level of prize money, high-profile judges and growing reputation have a direct impact on encouraging participation in our writing and visual arts awards. Meanwhile the Scottish Arts Trust Bursary Fund annually enables more than one hundred talented writers and artists to take part in our awards without paying entry fees.

The critical funding provided by our donors enables high-profile prizes and underpins the very ecosystem that makes the Scottish Arts Trust so unique. Activities we support include exhibitions at Scotland's leading arts venues; digital and online exhibitions; publications including exhibition catalogues and anthologies; films that reach tens of thousands around the world, talks and networking opportunities for artists and writers and performance opportunities for musicians and composers.

Our goal is for everyone to have the opportunity to showcase creativity. We welcome any contribution to help us on that journey. Learn more at www.scottishartstrust.org

Other publications from the Scottish Arts Trust

The Edinburgh Anthology Series

The Outlier and other stories, Edinburgh Anthology (Volume 1) Edited by Sara Cameron McBean and Claire Rocha (2024)

The Scottish Arts Club Story Awards Series

Solemates and other stories from the Scottish Arts Club Story Awards 2023 (Volume 5). Edited by Sara Cameron McBean and Claire Rocha (2023)

Beached and other stories from the Scottish Arts Club Story Awards 2022 (Volume 4). Edited by Sara Cameron McBean and Claire Rocha (2022)

A Meal for the Man in Tails and other stories from the Scottish Arts Club Story Awards 2021 (Volume 3). Edited by Sara Cameron McBean and Michael Hamish Glen (2021)

Life on the Margins and other stories from the Scottish Arts Trust Story Awards 2019-2020 (Volume 2). Edited by Sara Cameron McBean and Michael Hamish Glen (2020)

The Desperation Game and other stories from the Scottish Arts Trust Story Awards 2014-2018 (Volume 1). Edited by Sara Cameron McBean and Hilary Munro (2019)

Other titles

Rosalka: The Silkie Woman and other stories, plays and poems by Isobel Lodge (2018)

Praise from the judges

Edinburgh Short Story Award 2025
From judges Christopher Brookmyre and Marissa Haetzman

On the winning story, *The Scapegoat* by Jacob Ashton
> *This is a meticulously well-crafted story... that subverts expectations, sending us down an unforeseen path. The prose is of an exceptionally high quality, with some eminently quotable turns of phrase.*

On *The Winter Visitor at Garve Station* by Duncan MacInnes, Second Prize
> *This is a beautifully realised story, full of melancholy, tenderness and loss... The prose is both refined and elegiac. An exquisite piece of writing.*

On *Cloth Man* by Julie May Noteman, Third Prize and winner of the First Write Award for Unpublished Writers Worldwide
> *This is a small but significant drama brought to life by a skilful use of place and setting... an effective call for kindness in a hostile world.*

On *Heartsick* by Rachael Cameron, winner of the Isobel Lodge Award for Unpublished Writers in Scotland.
> *A highly original, visceral and at times shocking meditation on the ravages of grief...*

Edinburgh Flash Fiction Awards
From judge Meg Pokrass

On the winning story, *Wild Horses* by Cecilia Maddison
> *'Wild Horses' is a flash that I couldn't unstick from my heart. The author teaches us how the use of blended metaphor can add a magical element to an otherwise realistic scenario.*

On *The Great Ivories* by Alexandra Lane, Second Prize
> *In 'The Great Ivories' the author weaves themes of ecocide, anthropocentrism and threatened extinction with a deftness of touch. I was amazed by the beautiful imagery and how deep themes were handled in this compressed form.*

On *War Bride* by Judith Allnatt, Third Prize
> *'War Bride' is a devastating, poetically written tale about the impossible effects of wartime PTSD.*

On *Homesickly* by Margaret McMillan, Golden Hare Award winner
> *'Homesickly' is a gently mocking, deadpan funny snapshot of a ward round in a London teaching hospital… The dialogue is hilariously funny.*

Edinburgh True Flash Awards
From judge Meg Pokrass

On the winning story *All That Time* by Sophie Olszowski

> *An evocative piece of… the author has a gift for emotional detail… We come to feel what the narrator feels, and are left with the surprise of hope.*

Edinburgh Writing Awards

scottishartstrust.org/writing

Edinburgh Short Story Award

Open to writers worldwide and stories on any topic up to 2,000 words. Enter from 1 November to 28 February annually

- First Prize £1,000, Second Prize £500, Third Prize £250
- The Isobel Lodge Award (£750) for top short story entered by an unpublished writer living in Scotland
- The Write Mango Award (£300) for the most amusing, bizarre story
- The First Write Award (£300) for the top story by an unpublished writer, worldwide
- Authors of the top 15 short stories are offered publication in the Edinburgh Anthology

Edinburgh Flash Fiction Award

Open to writers worldwide and stories on any topic up to 250 words. Enter from 1 May to 31 August annually

- First Prize £1,000, Second Prize £500, Third Prize £250
- The Golden Hare Award (£500) is for the top flash fiction entry by a writer living in Scotland
- The Write Mango Flash Award (£300) for the most amusing, bizarre story
- Authors of the top 15 flash fiction stories are offered publication in the Edinburgh Anthology

Edinburgh Essay Award

For writers worldwide and essays on any topic up to 2,000 words. Enter from 1 November to 10 March annually

- First Prize £1,000, Second Prize £500, Third Prize £250
- Authors of the top 15 essays are offered publication in the Edinburgh Anthology

Edinburgh Novel Award

For writers worldwide and novels in any genre. Enter from 1 November to 10 March annually

- First Prize £1,500, Second Prize £500, Third Prize £250

Edinburgh Young Adult Novel Award

For writers worldwide and novels or graphic novels suitable for readers age 12 and older. Enter from 1 November to 10 March annually

- First Prize £1,500, Second Prize £500, Third Prize £250

Edinburgh True Flash Award

For writers worldwide and true stories up to 250 words.

- First Prize £500, 2 Commendations £100 each

Contents

Edinburgh Short Story Awards 2025

First Prize
Jacob Ashton, *The Scapegoat*

Second Prize
Duncan MacInnes, *The Winter Visitor at Garve Station*

Third Prize and **First Write Award for Unpublished Writers Worldwide**
Julie-May Noteman, *Cloth Man*

Isobel Lodge Award for Unpublished Writers in Scotland
Rachael Cameron, *Heartsick*

Write Mango Short Story Award
Angela Drinnan, *Medusa Goes to the Hairdresser*

Highly Commended
Racheal Jones, *Nincompoop Cures Cancer*
Sarah Rigby, *Square Lives*

Editor's Choice
Saira Arian, *Bhutto is Dead*

Reader's Choice
These stories were notable favourites among our readers

Ralph Bolland, *All Not Breathing*
Holly Brandon, *God Bless Fried Chicken at Clucker's Sunday Lunch*

Kája Kubičková, *Fermenting*
Genevieve Flintham, *Locusts and Dragons*
Katy Walker, *Chicken Bones*

The Scapegoat

by Jacob Ashton

First Prize, Edinburgh Short Story Award 2025

The three of us were 'young professionals', up-and-coming in the working world, financial stability perhaps only a decade away. Magda managed a branch of a tapas chain that masqueraded as homespun and wholesome through sepia prints of local landmarks and jars of preserved garlic. Vick designed asset management software for hedge funds, a niche made lucrative through a heady cocktail of dubious ethics and excruciating tedium. I worked as a consultant ecologist, advising property developers on whether the beasts and bugs nestled in the greenfield sites in their sights were deemed commonplace enough to merit their destruction. In theory, all of us had solid, well-paid jobs – but we had made the critical error of living in a moderately not-horrible city in an era of eye-watering rent. Living solo was financial suicide.

So, we had maintained the marginally more affordable option of a house share and reluctantly persevered with the challenges of communal living, cursed to endlessly negotiate differences of opinion on standards of cleanliness, definitions of room temperature, and whether it's acceptable to boil chicken soup in the kitchen kettle. But the rent was cheap, relatively speaking, so we had set aside our differences to find a mutually acceptable approach to conflict resolution. Which is why we invented Nadine.

Nadine was the household's only sinner and, through this selfless sacrifice, absolved the rest of us of all our wrongdoings. Us three, on the other hand, were model housemates without a fault to our names. In this way, harmony was maintained. Any gripes or grievances could be aired freely, as Nadine was inevitably the culprit:

'I wonder if Nadine knows it's her turn to clean the fridge?'

'If you see Nadine, could you ask her to stop scraping the non-stick pans?'

'Nadine's left something truly unholy in the toilet – but I'm sure she'll sort it out soon.'

The house formed one segment of a decaying Victorian terrace, originally one bedroom but, with some canny retrofitting – namely, gutting and converting the 'non-essential' living room and one bathroom – made to house three. Occasional half-hearted maintenance efforts by the landlord kept it just within liveable conditions. The radiators worked with a few hours' notice; the windows kept the heat in if the edges were stuffed with rags (thoughtfully left behind by past tenants); and by placing a paving slab on the washing machine, its trail of destruction round the kitchen could be mostly mitigated. The house had even been repainted within living memory, an uneven layer of Eggshell White coating walls, doors, doorknobs, and a smattering of squashed insects.

Nadine 'lived' behind the locked door on the upstairs landing. The room beyond presumably housed the landlord's neglected refurbishment materials, or maybe the boiler. Nothing that concerned us tenants, anyway. Under the guise of the portal to Nadine's abode, the door became a sticky note metropolis: a public forum to put forward suggestions for more harmonious housematery in writing.

'Hi Nadine, please could you clean your hair trimmings from the sink?'

'Nadine – quick reminder that if the milk has someone else's name written on it, that means it's theirs, not yours :)'

'Hi Nadine, so happy your love life is going strong, but please keep the decibels down after midnight, thanks x'

Nadine formed the core of our camaraderie. We were three very different people grudgingly sharing the same small space, but with one ultimate goal in common: to keep the house as peaceful as possible until we could hoard enough capital to escape to more hospitable climes. By rallying against the antisocial Nadine, it worked.

The first crack in our facade appeared when I arrived home late one night after a particularly brutal assignment. While surveying a lush wildflower-laden meadow, ripe for conversion to another out-of-town shopping centre, I had stumbled upon a protected species of bat roosting in an oak tree. My account of this rarity was not met positively; the developer had charmingly offered to set both the tree and my house on fire if the report was not retracted. When I went to leave, the slashed tyre on my car seemed unlikely to be a coincidence.

It was well into the small hours when I finally made it home, so I slipped in quietly, using my survey torch to light my way. Reaching the upstairs landing, an almost-inaudible creak reached me. A movement, caught in the torchlight: Nadine's door closed shut with a click.

For a moment, I wondered if I'd imagined it. To my knowledge, the door had never been opened during our tenure. I approached the door, thinking to test the handle, but paused. Surely there was a less confrontational way of addressing the mystery.

Instead, I treated the door to a new addition to its sticky note community:

'Hi Nadine, did you have your door open around 2am? Just checking all's good?'

That should cover it. I headed to bed.

The next morning, the sticky note had a response in scratchy handwriting:

'I was just thirsty.'

Magda and Vick were both in the kitchen when I entered, comfortably ignoring each other as they prepared themselves for work. Vick was scarfing down cereal as he scrutinised a nefarious-looking block of code on his laptop. Magda was making a cup of tea while bobbing along to the trance track that issued faintly from her headphones.

I asked Vick if he'd heard anything strange last night.

'Just the normal,' he said, raising his eyebrows conspiratorially.

'No, not Magda's night guest –,'

'You mean Nadine's.' Vick pressed a single key on his keyboard and a chunk of code turned red. He swore softly.

'No. I mean, yes. I mean, from the room with the sticky notes.'

'Maybe the boiler's playing up. There was no hot water this morning. I assumed Nadine used it all again.' He glanced at Magda, whose hair was wrapped in a towel. She was frowning at her phone, blissfully unaware of Vick's remarks.

'Ghosted again,' she muttered to herself, staring at the little screen as if willing a notification to appear. 'Men only want one thing.' Vick rolled his eyes.

I looked down at the sticky note in my hand. Magda's handwriting was large and loopy, while Vick's was tight and blocky. The scratchy scrawl on the note matched neither.

'Hi Nadine, wondering if you can sort out that funky smell? Thanks!'

Weeks passed but I couldn't shake the feeling of unease. Nadine's door stayed staidly shut, locked tight. The house was old, our tenancy just a footnote in its long history, and somehow I felt the building was keeping something from us – or, didn't consider us significant enough to share its secrets. Nadine's crimes continued unabated but the atmosphere remained hypnotically tranquil. The only noticeable change was the arrival of an odd sweetly metallic smell that occasionally permeated the landing.

Then one Friday, I returned from an evening in the pub to find both Vick and Magda in the kitchen, looking serious.

'We need to talk about Nadine,' said Vick.

'What's she done now?' I asked, trying to sound sober.

He placed a sticky note on the table.

'Nadine, have you paid your share of the rent? The landlord says someone hasn't paid.'

The question was in Vick's handwriting. And underneath, a scratchy reply:

'Sorry, I'm a bit short. Can you cover me this month? I'll pay back asap.'

'Could you talk to Nadine and tell her she needs to pay?' Magda asked. 'We're not covering her.' I realised both of them were looking at me intently.

'Wait, you think it's me that hasn't paid?' I said.

'No, of course not,' said Vick placatingly. 'It's Nadine.'

I nodded hesitantly, striving to clear the cider clouding my cerebral cortex.

'Great,' said Magda, smiling thinly. 'So if she could pay by tomorrow, that'd be perfect.'

'Wait. Wait. I mean, it's really not me.' I tried to find the words to explain but they stayed stubbornly hidden. 'Look.' I headed for the stairs, taking the sticky note with me. They reluctantly followed me to Nadine's door.

'That's my handwriting, there.' I pointed to a note reading:

'Hi Nadine, are you using my toothbrush? The purple one. Please don't!!!'

'It's different from this note. Right?' I looked pleadingly at Vick and Magda. My own sanity seemed at stake. Blessedly, I saw comprehension – and consequential confusion – dawning on their faces.

'But it's not my writing either, or Vick's,' said Magda. 'So who wrote it?'

'Could it be one of your – sorry, Nadine's – one-night stands?' said Vick.

'They wouldn't be one-night stands if they ever returned my messages,' said Magda bitterly. 'But no, it couldn't be. Nobody's come over since last week.'

None of us spoke for some moments.

I slowly extended a hand to the door, silently willing them to stop me. They didn't. I knocked.

'Nadine?' I said, hating the crack in my voice. 'Sorry to disturb you. It's about the rent.'

We waited. Silence. Then, a subtle sound of shuffling. We all took a step back.

A click. The handle turned. Vick grabbed a coat hanger from the drying rack, presumably for self defence.

The door opened a crack. From the darkness within, a pale, dark-haired young woman peered out.

'Hi guys,' she said. 'What's up?'

My heartbeat cranked up several notches. Vick emitted a weird little whimper.

'Nadine?' Magda croaked.

'I'll answer to anything.' Nadine stared impassively at the three of us.

'Who are you?' said Vick. 'What are you doing in our house?'

Nadine crossed her arms. 'I live here, Vick. I've lived here for years. You obviously know that.' She indicated the slew of sticky notes populating her door.

I felt queasy. The ciders were dancing a samba in my stomach.

'Sorry about the rent,' said Nadine. 'Everyone's cashless these days. But I'll pay you back next month, I promise.'

'No worries,' I said thickly.

'Actually, while I have you all, I've got a bone to pick,' said Nadine. 'Loads of these notes aren't anything to do with me.' She tore a handful of them from the door. 'I don't drink milk, I don't cook, I don't use the bathroom. Okay, the smell was my fault, granted, and I'm working on sorting it. But please stop accusing me of things I didn't do. It feels super aggressive.'

Magda began hyperventilating.

'So you've been here all this time?' she said between gasps. 'Why have we never seen you?'

'Different schedules. Different lifestyles. Different means of entry.' Her expression gave little away.

I frowned, fighting through the brain fog.

'Did you say you don't use the bathroom?' I said. 'Do you have like a… bucket in there?' The strange odour emanated from the dark room behind her, though it didn't smell lavatorial.

Nadine rolled her eyes.

'Vampires don't need to use the toilet, genius,' she said.

'You're a vampire?' said Vick, clutching the coat hanger tighter. I became painfully aware of my own empty hands.

'Obviously.' Nadine's top lip curled back to reveal shiny white fangs. 'But you can chill out. I don't eat housemates or their loved ones. There's a clause in the rental agreement. You'd know if you'd read it.'

'So what do you eat?' I asked. Morbid curiosity superseded fear.

Nadine shrugged. 'Whoever I find out and about in the night. The wealthier-looking ones normally, so I can make rent. Failing that, those weirdos that stumble about on the landing after a night with Magda.'

'You've been eating my dates?' Magda shrieked. 'That's why they never get back to me? Because they're dead?'

'Oh, sorry. I thought you'd done with them. You know, if it was an issue,' – Nadine gestured at her decorated door – 'Then you really should've left a note.'

The Winter Visitor at Garve Station

by Duncan MacInnes

Second Prize, Edinburgh Short Story Award 2025

Word came down the A87 that the hill at Cluanie had yet
to be cleared of snow, so all that was left to me that
morning was the Inverness train from Kyle of Lochalsh.
There's something about the station at Kyle which speaks
of endings, the way it's saved from the sea only by a wall
where the fishing boats gather, patient as mourners, the
way the rails quit suddenly as if they got to the edge of
Scotland and recoiled from the wild Atlantic.

Two carriages waited in the white dawn, both nearly
empty. Across the water, the mountains of Skye seemed
to float on a layer of mist. I boarded, and all was well at
first. The rail tracks curved in and around the coastal
bays of Wester Ross, as the sea crashed on their shores. I
saw from my window the rain-slicked road remained
black and bare and I suspected that yet again I had
listened too well to my *banshee* voice whispering of doom.

That morning, most of the other passengers left at
Plockton, wrestling their shopping bags onto the
platform, leaving only three men who looked like
climbers. By the time we approached Achnashellach
station, the snow had fallen again; already it was drifting
over the tracks and from the train's brakes came a
shrieking sound. We came to a halt, and the climbers got
to their feet. The ice axes and crampons suspended from

their rucksacks clinked and jingled as they moved off the train. Now there was only me and the unseen driver.

There's a particular ache I feel on the Highland Railway, one I've known since childhood. The train took me to military school, where they sent me after my soldier father's death. On these winter journeys I would wonder at the cleverness of people who'd invented ways to travel through a blighted, frozen landscape, one you knew was impossible to survive on your own. I got used to it in the end, to train journeys where the heating seldom worked, to a school where bugle calls mingled with the smell of cordite, to being alone.

The train rolled on through the ice-blasted glens, and as usual I thought about what would happen if I chose to step off the train as it slowed on one of the steep gradients, what would happen if I stood then in the snow, watching the cocoon of light and warmth speed away, away? I wondered, as my head began to nod to the tempo of the wheels on the railway cross-ties, if a cold, white death could be softened by the onset of sleep. I imagined it would come easily enough, gentle as a mother's hand.

I awoke when we clattered over a railway bridge and I saw two stags, twelve pointers both, leaping from their shelter, effortlessly bounding over the moor. It was then I switched on my camera, although too late for the deer, by now dwindling dots against the snow. The train rumbled on, its rhythm over the wilderness scored by Gaelic place-names; Achnasheen, Glencarron, Achanalt, Lochluichart. The last of these had a ghostly counterpart, under the waters of the dam built long ago, its wicker fence rotted, its spectral platform awaiting footsteps forever. These were stations where passengers boarded or disembarked by request, one of them only if the driver knew you. As if paying our respects, we slowed in passing their deserted platforms.

At last, a farmhouse came into view, the first outpost of the settled world. Scheduled stops began again and the first of these was Garve station. As we slowed to a halt, a single figure emerged on the platform, a young man, dressed in mountain gear; a woollen cap, black waterproof jacket and trousers. He looked fit, except that one leg was missing, the trousers pinned up above the knee. The man seemed almost heroic, his back erect like a soldier, supporting himself on crutches, while around his head the snowflakes flickered in the station lights.

Then he lifted his crutches and began to swing along the platform at speed, quick as youth itself. There was something in the way he moved, a loose thread in a memory, which reminded me of Terry, an old schoolfriend. It couldn't be him, of course, I reminded myself. As he swung by, I lifted the camera without thinking and clicked the shutter. It was intrusive, but I consoled myself that the train would soon be on its way.

Winter always brought Terry back to me. The day we met, he was sledging on a hillside, a new boy taking risks, showing off. When he hit a rock at the bottom, the blood from his nose left perfect red disks on the snow as he marched back up the hill. I knew to tilt his head back, to pack snow around his nostrils — the kind of knowledge you gather when you're sent away young. Before I had finished, he threw himself back onto the sledge, his wild yell echoing off the hills like joy itself. Something in that reckless abandon caught at my careful heart, and when he came back up again, I followed him down.

We were both fatherless boys, our inheritance the memory of men who died serving a decaying Empire. Terry chose the hot taste of life to fill the space; I chose books and silence. But that winter, we traded pieces of ourselves — my stillness for his motion, his wildness for my words. When I challenged him to choose a book from the library, he brought back 'The Worst Journey in the World' by Apsley Cherry-Garrard, a man perhaps too tender for the story he had to tell. It was a tale of Antarctic explorers seeking penguin eggs, of cold so fierce it could crack teeth, of the cruel responsibility given to one so young, waiting with sledges and dogs at One-Ton Camp for the doomed Scott expedition. Cherry-Garrard carried that load for the rest of his days, a stone lodged in his heart forever.

Looking back now, I wonder if Terry chose that book not just for its adventure, but as a gift to me – yes, nature might be dangerous, but it could be sweetened by beauty and laughter. From the book, he liked to quote, "Take it all in all, I do not believe anybody on earth has a worse time than an Emperor penguin." The absurdity caught us both, laughter spilling out like water, Terry falling back from his bed onto the dormitory floor, still laughing.

Later, I tried to match him with "The point, one begins to see, was to survive as English gentlemen," but it fell flat as a frozen cow-pat. Still, the next time we went sledging, Terry shouted it to the sky before hurling himself down the hill, turning my failed joke into something magnificent.

After school, we grew into the shapes we were always meant to fill. I disappeared into Edinburgh University's history library, while Terry followed Cherry-Garrard's themes of adventure and pluck, courtesy of the Royal Marines. When he left the Army, he became a winter climber of note, recognised for his exploits in the Scottish mountains and then the Alps. He never lost his appetite for risk and I never lost my appetite for reflection. The last time we saw each other, his arm was in a sling. I imagined my wounds were not so easily seen.

He spoke of Everest then, of climbing it alone, without oxygen – the kind of feat that would later make Reinhold Messner famous. But that day he cut short his enthusiasm because he could see how things were with me.

'You need to get up on these Skye hills,' he said. 'When I get back from the Himalayas, you and me, we'll go. It'll be like old times.'

The news came to me in an Edinburgh bar, casual as spilled beer. Terry had vanished from Everest base camp, walking away, away, into the eternal snow. They never found his body, but perhaps that was fitting. My friend in the bar spoke of the Himalayas' lost army of the dead, but Terry never belonged to the lost. He had such a passion for life that it was easier to assume he had jumped ship, so to speak, struck out for strange lands, or at least found some other world where the snow never stops falling and every hill points to heaven.

The train cleared its throat and began to move off from Garve, and apart from the hum of the diesel engine, there was silence in the carriage. So it was noticeable when a faint repetitive noise came from further along the train. It got closer and louder and, although it seemed incredible, what I was hearing was the tap, tap, tap of crutches. Seconds later, the one-legged man I'd photographed swung into view, threw his crutches into the corner opposite and, gripping the edge of the table, pivoted into the seat facing me.

I was a little shocked, not least at the speed with which he'd boarded the train. Also, given two empty carriages, that he'd chosen to sit opposite me. *He saw me taking the photograph and he'll ask me to delete it.* I didn't want to. It was the best I'd taken for ages; the snow moiling and gyrating around the platform, empty save for the single, almost martial figure under the overcast sky. *This could be embarrassing,* I thought as he stared at me. His face held echoes of Terry's, but I told myself it was just the light, just the snow, just the old grief playing tricks.

I looked out of the window, determined not to start the conversation. Nothing in the white flatlands rewarded my gaze apart from an occasional farmhouse. The man continued to stare.

I've never really had the mental strength to challenge or confront. I suppose that's why, despite getting my degree, I did nothing with it and still live on the island where I was born. Predictably, I relented.

'I'm glad I'm not out there,' I said, gesturing at the snow and the dark, threatening clouds. He waited a couple of seconds before he smiled, and I was relieved. Perhaps the problem had been in my head after all.

Then he leaned over the table and staring into my eyes, he quoted words I had last read thirty years ago. "They talk of the heroism of the dying – the little they know – it would be so easy to die, a dose of morphia, a friendly crevasse, and blissful sleep."

He was no longer smiling. "The trouble is to go on... "

He held my gaze for a full minute. Then, with a quick nod, he swivelled out of his seat, stood up, and adjusted his crutches. Staring down at me, he said, "If you march your winter journeys you will have your reward." He winked. "So long as all you want is a penguin's egg." Then he turned away, and I saw his shoulders begin to shake. He was laughing. As energetically as before, he sped off in the direction he had come.

I continued to sit for a couple of minutes, stunned by Cherry-Garrard's words echoing down the years. Then I got up and moved towards the rear of the train, all the way through my carriage and the next. As I stood looking at the empty seats, the tannoy sparked into life and the driver announced 'Next stop, Dingwall'. In desperation, I turned and raced back, remembering I'd failed to check the train's only toilet. It was empty, so I continued to the front of the train, where I arrived just as it slowed to a stop at Dingwall Station. I stuck my head out of the window and looked back along the platform. Of the one-legged man, there was no sign.

Cloth Man

by Julie-May Noteman

Third Prize, Edinburgh Short Story Award 2025
First Write Award 2025 for Unpublished Writers Worldwide

I am cloth-man. My hands dip and lift and dip and lift in
rhythmic perfection. Long sweeps, short sweeps, up and
down. I slap my cloth, sodden and dripping, onto the
windscreen and the water runs down my arm, cold as a
night with a sky full of stars, dip and lift and dip and lift.
The cars shunt forward waiting their turn, waiting for me
to slap my cloth and sweep my arm, long sweeps, short
sweeps, backwards and forwards.

The next car eases in beside me and I wait with my cloth
held high, ready for my moment. It is black, big and black
and my reflection merges into its sides as though I am
part of it. I am cold. My trousers hang against my long
legs and flap as the wind blows through. I am always
cold here. They have given me black rubber gloves that
shine with the wet and make my hands look fat and
puffed and slimy like the catfish from the Onitsha River.

The man inside this car is wide – I see his large shirt-
covered belly wedged behind the steering wheel. His face
is red as he shouts into the air in the sealed up car like a
mad man; his arms gesticulate as a voice answers back
from his connected phone. The man looks out of his
water-smeared window, straight at me, straight at my
face and my eyes but he does not see me as he talks into

the air. He looks straight through me as though I am a shadow. I slap my pink cloth over his face.

Others move around me, their skin different from mine, men whose language I do not know – clipped sounds, like the sounds of the grasshopper, lithe and efficient as they move from car to car. We speak in a language of nods and flicks and tilted chins, fingers that point and hands that beckon the cars forward.

The spray-man is beside me. This morning he showed me his country on a map on his phone. I pointed at mine and we stared at the great distance that was between them and at the great distance that is between them and here. He wears his rubber gloves and sprays the cars with fast jets of water that gush from the end of the thin metal pipe attached to a hose attached to a plastic barrel of water. A cigarette hangs from his mouth as he sprays the wheel hubs and the sides and the windows and the roof. I watch him move, the hose pipe whipping and winding after him like a cobra. The spray falls through the air, light and cold like the rain in this country – not like the rain at home that waits and waits, then explodes, heavy and warm and life-changing.

The man opens his window half down. I hold my cloth in one hand and it drips onto my foot. Spray-man stops the jet. He shouts at us through the gap in the window as though neither of us have ears that work.

'Mini-valet.'

I think back to Mr. Ibrahim standing beside his chalk board as we sat in our white shirts and blue shorts at wooden desks, shaded from the sun that blazed beyond the open door.

'In English you must say the word please when you ask for something.'

We would chant in unison as he pointed with his metre stick to the white words on the black board, 'Please may I have a mango?' 'Please may I go to the toilet?' 'Please can you help me?' We were made to stand, one by one beside our desks, and practise saying our names.

'My name is Ebuka Okelie,' I would call out towards the teacher, 'I am very pleased to meet you.'

I say nothing and the man stares at me as though I am stupid.

'Can you not speak English?' he barks.

I can speak English. Before Boko Harem closed our school, I was the best pupil in Mr Ibrahim's class but the English I learnt so diligently, words written in flowing script, sounds pronounced meticulously, is not the same as they speak here. The words in this place are quicker than a flood rushing down the dry hillside – squeezed together with no space to breathe or me to understand.

Pouch-man strides over. He smiles at the customers and carries the money in a belt around his waist; the money that will pay for my food; the money that will pay for my phone so that I can speak to my brother who is trying to get away; the money that I will save and send so he can escape the place where my parents and sister are no more. I wonder how much money is in that belt and suck in my lips and feel tears stinging in the corners of my eyes. Pouch-man is in charge because he speaks English better than anyone else. He shows his gold tooth as he smiles at the man in the black car.

'No problem sir,' he says, waving the big car forwards and down towards the mini-valet-women who squat on low stools in a circle around a vacuum cleaner as though they are warming themselves by a big cooking pot on a fire.

I imagine they are cooking brown Amala and green Ewedu Soup with deep red tomatoes for the stew, my mouth waters and I lick my lips at the thought as if it might be true. These women wait silently in padded coats, their trousers wrapped with long skirts, faces blank and round.

A second small blue car pulls in for mini-valet. Pouch-man clicks his fingers and the women rise from their circle like a swarm of bees. He lifts his chin towards me and nods at the black car. At home I wanted to be an engineer, to design vast bridges and straight wide roads but now I have been promoted to mini-valet-man and I feel a surge of pride. The large man squeezes from his car and strides away, talking on his phone, pacing backwards and forwards across the grey tarmac. I am given a soft yellow cloth so that I can polish the inside rims of his car doors and the dimpled surface below the windscreen. I lean into the car and let my hand move slowly and gently over the black shining metal, smooth and slender. I close my eyes and think of my beautiful Ifeoma back at home and picture myself cycling past her, showing off, standing on the pedals of my orange bike – no hands – her waving shyly and laughing her wonderful laugh. I wonder where she is and if I will ever see her again. As I wipe the window frame I look over at the lady who is waiting for her car to be cleaned. Pouch-man has given her a cup of tea in a white paper cup. Her yellow hair falls half over her white face. She is wearing a cream coat and sits very still on a white plastic chair reading a book. This lady reminds me of a long drink of goat's milk and the thought makes me laugh inside.

The black car is finished. I stand back, pleased with my work and turn my head to the side to admire the car that shines and gleams like a winner's trophy. The large man does not say thank you but pushes past me and stretches into the car across the driver's seat so that his trousers strain and slip from his bulk and his shirt rises up. His shout is loud and sudden and full of anger.

'He stole my money!'

He points at me with his fat finger and all the heads turn; the spray-man stops his spray and spits out his cigarette and stamps it slowly under his foot. I stand very still. I learnt to stand still when the men came with their guns and when I waited in the night for the lorry to come. I stand very still and do not speak.

'He stole my money,' he shouts again, moving towards me, menacing, aggressive, 'I had £20 sitting in that car.'

I understand all these words because he spits them slowly and carefully into my face. His spit mingles with the sweat which is beginning to form on my forehead.

'You people are all the same,' he growls like an animal and waves his arm towards the pouch-man and the spray-man and the mini-valet-women.

I expect the pouch-man to rush forwards, smiling, apologising telling this angry man that he is very sorry, very sorry indeed that this man would steal his money. But pouch-man does not move. I watch his fist tighten at his side. Out of the corner of my eye I see spray-man to my left and sense the mini-valet women move closer to me, warm like a blanket, the sway of their hips, the shuffle of their feet, the softness of their noise as they wrap their arms and clutch their spray bottles close to their chests. A bus rumbles up the road. The milk-lady rises slowly from her seat and carefully sets her book and cup of tea down. She walks past me, past the mini-valet-women, past spray-man and pouch-man to a pool of soapy water lying on the ground beyond the black car. There is a moment that passes between us all, as short as a gunshot, as long as an endless journey as she bends down and puts her pale hand in the dark suds.

'I think this is your money,' she says to the large man, pulling something slippery and wet from the water. 'You must have dropped it.'

Pouch-man rushes forwards and takes the money. 'Mini-valet, £20, thank you very much sir.' Pouch-man does not smile at the large man with the black car but slowly shakes the money dry and puts it carefully into his money belt, then turns his back and walks away.

The rest of us stand bunched beside the milk-lady and watch as the man reverses his shining car, then revs it forwards, the loose gravel spitting and crunching as the car squeals out onto the main road. The milk-lady turns to me.

'My name is Heather,' she says and reaches her hand towards me and smiles right into my eyes.

I hold tight to this hand because it is the first hand I have held since I arrived. 'My name is Ebuka Okelie,' I say, with my head held high, 'I am very pleased to meet you.'

Spray-man nudges me and puts out his hand, 'My name is Amir Karim.'

The pouch-man calls for a tea break.

There is a pause, a gentle sigh, before he adds in a voice so quiet and low that we lean forward to hear, 'My name is Nikolai.'

Then, like fizz from a bottle that has been shaken and held too long the noise begins to seep out of us, many dialects and voices and sounds erupting into chatter and laughter, great belly laughs that make the mini-valet women shake all over and now names are being called backwards and forwards across the tarmac and over white paper cups of tea, Elena, Maria, Brigita, Tatiana, Minka and the sound rises like the beautiful sound of morning birds in the tall Kapok tree. The thought makes me look up and around as if these birds might be high in the grey skies. I breathe in, a long deep breath and squeeze my yellow cloth. The rain has stopped and I no longer feel cold. From behind a cloud a small hint of sun begins to peep.

Heartsick

by Rachael Cameron

Winner, Isobel Lodge Award 2025 for Unpublished Writers in Scotland

The studio is different to all the others. Its walls are white and clinical, covered in official-looking posters written in angry red typeface. Warnings, like the ones you see on cigarette packages threatening the ruin of your lungs; *proceed at own risk*. None of the grungy decadent glamour she's used to, no offbeat art and knickknacks, no gothic overtones and Chesterfield sofas. Here it's all disclaimers and terms and conditions; so much more official than you'd expect a tattoo place to be.

But, she supposes, this isn't just any tattoo place. That's the point.

Her skin already crawls with artwork. She's a piece of land claimed by so many talented hands; they fight for space across her body's topography. Tattoos jostle for premium territory, turf wars erupt between sacred hearts and dragons and ornamental flowers. There's no theme, no cohesion, simply a collection of art for art's sake. It's never really meant anything deeper, until now.

It's hard to find pieces of her that remain unadorned. Glimpses of white skin between black lines, the apples of her cheeks rosy and bare.

She has no more space on the outside.

The front door of the shop closes behind her as she rings the bell on the gleaming white counter. The smell of antiseptic hangs in the air.

An older man emerges from behind the counter, and he's not what she expected, either. He wears a suit and tie and has the briskly professional attitude of a businessman, or maybe a surgeon. Yes, that would be more fitting – everything about this place screams *medical*. The only clue that he's in any way unconventional are the twin swallows etched on his hands. A lump forms in her throat. He reminds her of her dad.

'Can I help you?'

'Hi, yeah I have a booking at 11? Lia Jones.'

'Ah right, hi – I'm Barry, nice to meet you,' he says, extending his hand formally for her to shake. 'Did you already fill out the forms and sign the waiver?'

She nods.

'Cool, bear with me a minute to get set up and I'll be right with you. Feel free to take a look through the portfolio while you're waiting.' He gestures to two large leather binders and disappears back into the other room.

She flicks through the first portfolio; pieces of work that start off mundane and become more interesting only because of the surfaces on which they're inked. Uninspired, her stomach beginning to sink, she turns to the second binder.

The images take her breath away. Whisper-fine linework, colour that soars off the page to strike right in the gut. Talent that is refined, polished, but also raw and dynamic. This is what she needs, the only thing that will work.

'See anything you like?'

'Yeah, actually,' she says, 'this is exactly what I'm looking for.'

Barry leans over to inspect the photo, his features settling into a frown.

'I'm sorry, I should have said which portfolio to look at. This isn't my work I'm afraid, it's my apprentice's.'

'Oh right, is he here today? And available?'

'He's here, but I'm sorry, it's not going to be possible for him to tattoo you.'

'Oh, okay,' she says, disappointed. 'I'm sorry to mess you around, I know I was booked in with you today, but… Could I rebook for a day he's free?'

Barry's frown deepens.

'Sorry, but I don't think you're understanding me. He's not able to tattoo in this particular medium yet. You'll see from his portfolio that all of his work, to date, has been on skin only.'

She hadn't noticed that, but it doesn't faze her.

'Well,' she begins, tentatively. 'I'd be happy to take the risk, and I guess he'll need to learn on someone, right?'

Lia meets the apprentice fifteen minutes later, Barry a disapproving presence in the background as they discuss what she wants. The apprentice's name is Sean and he's only a couple of years older than she is, probably late twenties, and he is every bit the tattoo artist cliché she'd come looking for. Dishevelled and stubble-jawed, he smells of stale smoke even above the antiseptic stench in the shop. He reeks of heartbreak and casual sex.

Barry is still trying to talk them both out of this.

'You have to understand what it is you're getting into,' he warns, again. 'It's not as simple as surface-level stuff, there's bigger things at play here. Sean hasn't achieved the distance to do this; he could leave a completely different mark on you than the one you're expecting.'

'Hey, man,' Sean interjects, palms raised in supplication. 'I feel ready. I feel good about this. It'll be cool, yeah?'

Barry's patience gives out.

'It's not about how you feel! It's about the danger of creating a connection, a bond. Leaving a trace of yourself behind in her. Can you be certain you can close yourself down the entire time you're working? Not lose focus, even once?'

'I'm ready, man.'

It's chilly in the room with her top off. The hard tattoo bed is not comfortable, and each individual vertebrae of her spine presses into the clingfilm-wrapped leather. Breathing deeply, she clamps down on her nerves as Sean approaches with an injection of local anaesthetic.

He asks Lia if she wants a mirror to watch him work, and she nods, unable to speak. When he's satisfied that she can feel nothing below the neck, he takes a wickedly sharp scalpel and makes a swift, deep incision from her collarbone to the bottom of her ribcage.

'Okay down there?' he asks.

'Yeah, I – I'm fine so far,' she replies, voice fraying.

'This next bit is what most people find the hardest,' he says. 'You might want to look away.'

Lia listens to him, screwing her eyes up tight. But there's no escaping the sounds, the grating, raucous cracking as he splits her ribcage into two halves. She is cracked open, quite literally; exposed in the most fundamental of ways.

A few moments pass in silence, until the rhythmic sound of the tattoo machine fills it. It's comforting in its familiarity, and with it her confidence returns enough to watch as Sean reaches into her open chest cavity, machine poised above the wet, gleaming ruby of her heart.

His eyes flick up, confirming that she's ready. He lowers the machine. Begins. Needle meets flesh and both of them breathe again only when the first stroke is complete.

Even with the anaesthetic, the vibrations ricochet all through her. There's no escaping the feel of his hands inside her ribcage, the knowledge that she has handed over all her power to him; he could destroy her, if he chose. The scent of burning flesh reaches her, iron-rich and meaty. Stroke after stroke he lines, free-handing the design. She watches it take shape in the mirror, focusing on the elegance of his hands covered in her blood. They are sleek white foxes, moving deftly through the red forest of her.

The process is transcendent, and ugly, and exhilarating. It is fire, a baptism, a sacred rite.

Barry's golden rule is that they're not allowed to speak, but Lia finds her story trickling out of her, as if the breaching of her body is more than simply physical. A leak has been opened through which her deepest self spills, until Sean catches it in his gloved palms. He cradles her pain tenderly, holding it close as precious jewels, as manna. He watches her grief trickle and then pour from her, his rockstar insouciance evaporating, making way for something between them that is both fragile and true.

Her father's face shimmers in the air between them, summoned into existence by the memorial Sean is carving into her heart's walls. It's only been a few weeks since his death and it's still raw enough to blister.

A surface-level tattoo would have buckled under the weight of this design. Everyday skin would be too meaningless, too mundane to hold it. But the heart is a muscle, it's strong enough to carry the wound. It's the last uncharted territory in her body, and that's the final gift she can offer her beloved dad. She talks about him as Sean works, memories spilling from her tongue.

Sean continues working; hours pass. He treats her heart with reverence and respect, a covetousness that pleases her. He reciprocates her truth-telling, and they pass between them nuggets of past, gathering each deep, rusty secret to polish with the other's shock or sympathy or laughter. Intimate, dangerous secrets that create an artificial bond; she tries to remember that this connection exists only in this time and place – it can only be temporary. Yet it doesn't feel artificial, or temporary, when her heart lies exposed between them. Maybe that's the danger.

When it's done, Sean closes Lia's chest carefully. It feels hollowed without his presence.

He runs through the aftercare, telling her what to expect through the healing process, and they emerge back into the front of the shop.

Barry waits for them. His head swings between her and Sean, examining.

'I told you not to create a connection,' he sighs, wearily. 'Well. You're both fucked.'

Her heart heals slowly. Her grief has assumed a different texture, the blade of it blunted slightly by the new tattoo and the catharsis of the procedure. Not easier, never easier, but softer. More malleable.

Barry's parting words had concerned her, but she dismissed it. He was clearly peeved at being passed over for his apprentice; his ego fractured enough to cast out shards. And if Lia experiences an ache in her heart, an ache that tugs her in the direction of the tattoo shop, it can only be coincidental.

She's seen Sean exactly three times since the tattoo. Well, she's spoken to him three times. She's *seen* him more often. When she watches him leave his flat and follows him to the train station. When she happens to grab coffee at the place opposite the tattoo shop. When she sees him standing outside her window, late at night, his eyes glinting darkly under the streetlights. The pain in her chest is less, in those moments. To be near him is to alleviate the ache.

It's beautiful. It's unbearable. It wasn't supposed to happen.

The insomnia begins after a couple of weeks. The burn in her heart is too intense to allow sleep; night after night, she finds herself pacing unfamiliar streets. She walks until her heart eases, and she knows that means he's close. When she sees him in daylight, the same purple crescents underline his eyes. His bewildered expression mirrors hers.

When neither of them can withstand the distance, they drift together, just for the relief that closeness brings. Their hands twitch towards each other's bodies, drawn not by want or attraction, or even friendship, but by an irresistible force that has Lia wanting to crawl under Sean's skin and make his body her home. They barely know one another, but he's seen her heart, she's offered him her grief. They're bonded, however unwillingly.

Weeks pass with no sleep; Lia moves into Sean's small flat, but soon even constant touch doesn't relieve the burn of craving. They try sex, only once, in desperation rather than desire, but even with their bodies joined it's impossible to get close enough.

There's only one solution; they both know it. Barry was right to warn them.

When Sean leans over her, scalpel in shaking hand, Lia smiles. Once more, he opens her, and the rot hits both of them instantly. The tattooed heart sits snugly in her ribcage, but it's no longer thriving. It's dull, crusted over where the lines meet, oozing foul-smelling liquid that coats her lungs and oesophagus. Her grief, having tried to force its way into Sean, has curdled.

'I'm sorry,' he whispers.

'Don't be,' she says softly. 'It had to be this way.'

He makes the cut.

Medusa Goes to the Hairdresser

by Angela Drinnan

Winner, Write Mango Short Story Award 2025

She saunters in, a shimmer of asps. Heads swivel.

'I have an appointment.' Her voice has the rasp of a heavy smoker.

Sally, the receptionist, avoids meeting her eye as she checks the bookings.

'Is it *Maddy* at 2?'

'That's me.' There's an edge to her, believe me, you wouldn't challenge her. Sally didn't.

'Take a seat, Saskia will be with you shortly.' Sally arranges her face into a smile.

As Medusa plonks herself down on the leather sofa, the snakes uncurl, relaxing around her shoulders. She takes her phone from the pocket of her jeans and starts to scroll, nails clacking.

Heads swivel back, eyes meeting each other's in the mirrors – the women want to laugh but they're too scared.

Saskia returns in a cloud of sweet apple from a vape break, giving Sally a grin on the front desk.

'Your two o'clock is here,' says Sally, her eyes brimming with meaning.

'So, what are we doing today?' Saskia asks as she moves Medusa to sit in front of the mirror. Saskia eyes the nest of vipers, not touching, but admiring their emerald vibrancy.

'I just need a change.' Medusa speaks quietly, not wanting to wake the snakes who are dozing now.

'Okay. A restyle then.'

'I was thinking…' Medusa holds up her phone to show an image of a closely cropped head.

Saskia steels herself, 'I don't think that look will work with your... hair.'

Medusa's shoulders sag with disappointment. The snakes stir, exhaling a sleepy sigh.

'What would you recommend then?'

'May I…?' Saskia reaches out a hand, questioningly.

'Oh sure, they won't bite. If you're gentle.'

Slowly, Saskia makes contact with snakeskin, fingers dusting the surface, surprised at their dryness. She remembers to breathe. Traces their length, cords of sinew.

'I wonder...'

'Yes?'

'I wonder about ringlets?'

The whole salon falls silent, watching for Medusa's reaction.

'Ringlets?

'I think if we coiled them tightly it would make the length more manageable – framing your face without losing the bounce.'

'You mean, not cutting?'

Saskia glances down at her scissors, recognising their limitations. 'Yeah, without needing to cut.'

There is a beat when their eyes meet in the mirror; Saskia realises she's stopped breathing again.

'Well…' Medusa shifts in her seat, turning her head as she imagines wearing ringlets. A smile plays around her mouth. 'Do you mean like Beyoncé?'

'Yes! Like Beyoncé.'

A giggle escapes the lips of one of the half-highlighted heads along the row. Medusa stiffens; the snakes rise, alert.

'Who laughed?'

Nobody owns up, but the flushed cheeks of the woman seeking to cover her grey with buttery caramel give her away. Medusa turns to look at her. Twenty-two snake heads glide towards her, tongues flicking, tasting her scent.

The woman positioned between Medusa and the giggler gets up, backs away. The cloud of hissing heads stretches out to fill the space. At the point of maximum elongation, they are just inches away from the culprit's face.

'I… I'm sorry,' she stammers. It doesn't seem enough. She repeats her apology, more emphatically – it has no impact on Medusa.

The serpents strain, tugging Medusa's head towards their prey. One of them is particularly exercised, contracting then extending its body repeatedly. It seems to be pointing, indicating the neck of the giggler. Glistening against her skin lies a golden chain, with some gem or trinket dangling into her cleavage.

Medusa smiles, her lips shining with gloss. 'Yes, give it to me.'

Flustered, not knowing what snakehead is referring to, she looks down. 'Oh, my chain, yes, take it. A gift, for you, I mean.' She fumbles with the clasp, looks to someone to help her out. One of the stylists steps forward and, hands shaking, undoes the catch. She passes the necklace to its owner, not wanting to be responsible for the handover.

Medusa holds out her hands to receive the offering. 'Why, thank you. So kind.' Her smile more of a grimace.

The woman edges closer to deposit her jewellery, not knowing how to safely penetrate the snake shield.

'Boys, at ease,' Medusa commands her snakes. They flop around her shoulders, the pointer the last to relax.

She manages to drop the chain into the bowl of Medusa's hands without touching her, then retreats, without turning her back. She does not return to her seat. She backs her way to the door, hair dye and all, leaving her jacket, which she never comes back to collect.

Medusa eyes her trophy approvingly. 'Would you mind?'

She holds it up to Saskia who fastens it around the neck of its new owner, the snakes parting obligingly. Medusa

52

nods her approval. 'I'm ready now. For ringlets. Like Beyoncé,' she adds, looking round the room in challenge.

All eyes are down. Nobody laughs.

Saskia dips her fingers into unctuous pomade and massages the serpents. They sigh with contentment, most of them nodding off. As the snakes relax, so does Medusa. Saskia teases their lithe bodies into coils. They seem to like it, as if it tickles. She swears she hears them chuckling. The other customers no longer fear for their lives, chatting resumes in the background, quietly, so as not to upset the salon's special guest. But they make a note to frequent a different establishment for their next trim. Saskia has rather enjoyed her contact with the snakes. The head rubs always were her favourite bit of the job. Perhaps she should do that massage course she'd always fancied?

Sally was picking at her nails on the front desk, wondering what to do when it came to charging Medusa. Should she charge for a restyle or was it insanity to think of asking for payment?

'Well, I think that's us for today Maddy.' Saskia holds up a mirror to the back of Medusa's head so she could see the results. Not only was Saskia holding her breath, she was clenching every muscle in her body.

Medusa claps her hands in delight like a mediaeval queen at court, turning her head from side to side, admiring her new look. She rises to her feet with a bounce, as if lighter.

'I'll give you the rest of this wax, apply it whenever you need a little lustre.'

'And this is for you. Just in case you ever need it.' Medusa hands Saskia a tiny blue glass vial, and then she walks out the door. Sally needn't have worried, it was evident there would be no bill.

Saskia looks down at the bottle in her hands and read the calligraphed lettering: anti-venom.

Nincompoop Cures Cancer

by Racheal Jones

Highly Commended, Edinburgh Short Story Award 2025

'I need some unicorn tears,' the woman said. 'And thank you for not telling security I was hiding behind that donkey.'

From his bench four stalls down, Adam stared at the trespasser who stood in the centre of the stable.

She looked like an Edwardian librarian who'd tumbled out of a haystack – upswept billows of auburn hair, spectacles, and straw poking out of every tailored pocket. She wasn't the first person to sneak onto Rainbow Farm, wanting something from a unicorn. At least once a month, a millionaire tried to hire Mathilda to jump out of a giant, fake cake at their daughter's birthday party.

There was nothing sadder than fake cake.

Except believing that a being as sacred and powerful as a unicorn belonged in the party aisle with confetti and balloons.

'My name is Lily Bly,' the woman said. 'Dr. Lily Bly, I suppose, but I'm not persnickety about the title.' She pulled an empty glass vial from her skirt pocket. It glinted in the sunlight beaming through the stable's high windows. 'An ounce of tears should do. For preliminary tests.'

'No,' Adam said.

'Ha! I knew you'd say that, being a big, strong – I mean, protective unicorn guardian, but what you don't know…' Her pretty brown eyes held a hint of lunacy. 'What you don't know is that I need unicorn tears to cure *cancer*.'

'No.'

'Oh.'

Adam almost smiled when she stopped at one syllable. She'd spoken more words in the last minute than he had all week. He continued carving a Sugar Bee apple with a toothpick. Swirling patterns and woodland scenes always made Mathilda happy, especially if they included a rabbit.

'I thought the whole curing-cancer thing would work on anyone,' Dr. Bly said, walking closer. 'Even Unicorn Batman. That's what they call you, you know, since you always wear black and don't say much and are all tall and heroic. I mean, stoic.'

She wants to hug you, Mathilda's musical voice resonated inside his head.

Unicorn Batman doesn't hug, he thought. He glanced into her stall. She was disguised as a chestnut mare.

'Dr. Bly,' Adam said. 'I won't allow anyone to make a unicorn cry.'

Not even to save poor, little, bald babies dying of cancer?

Damn, Mathilda.

Language, Adam.

'Okay,' the doctor said. 'That's fair. Let me think.'

She paced the aisle twice before pointing at his apple. 'You're an artist. An apple da Vinci. I believe that sweet donkey wants some apple. May I take the curly strip?'

Adam nodded.

'What's her name?'

'Hazel.'

'Excuse me. Hazel, sweetheart, I've got a treat for you.'

Hold onto your dumplings, Mathilda said. *I'm about to predict the future.*

Adam grunted, indicating his dumplings were held.

Lily has a PhD in something medieval-ish. She's found or translated a manuscript thought lost to time, written by a Dominican nun. It reveals how unicorn tears mixed with other ingredients can 'banish the wolf', which is medieval-speak for curing cancer.

The wolf?

Because cancer eats the body. I'm glad someone found the manuscript, and I will be volunteering my tears, but that doesn't mean I have to be sad. Lily will realize this in four seconds. When she asks you a question, answer 'silly-sounding words'.

What?

Silly-sounding words, like nincompoop.

'I've got it,' Lily cried out, running back to Adam. 'People don't just cry when they're sad. They cry for joy. They laugh so hard they cry. Is it the same for unicorns? What do they find amusing?'

'Silly-sounding words.'

'In what language?'

'Any.'

'So, words like… absquatulate?'

That's a silly word, Mathilda said with a snort. Lily heard the snort and saw the chestnut mare in the stall.

'What a beautiful horse. What's her name?'

'Mathilda'

'Hello, Mathilda. Pleased to meet you.'

Hello, Lily. Adam, tell her I said hello and that you want to hug her, too.

No.

You're a nincompoop.

'This is good,' Lily said, tucking the glass vial back into her pocket. 'I know many silly words. Bumfuzzle, doohickey, mollycoddle, spleenwort. That's a type of fern. And I can research more. May I return tomorrow?'

'I'll add you to the guest list, so you don't have to dive into Hazel's stall again.'

Seventeen words, Adam? Seventeen whole words? You really are crushing on her.

The next day, Lily didn't look like an Edwardian librarian. She looked like an Edwardian cheerleader. She wore her spectacles, a full tweed skirt, a sweater emblazoned with a red H, and flat-heeled boots. She'd wound her auburn braids into two buns that looked like mouse ears. She carried a piece of paper and a large megaphone.

Adam ignored how his heartbeat raced at the absurd sight of her.

'Good morning,' she said, handing him the paper. 'That's a list of the today's silly words, with definitions. I wish I were fluent in more languages. I don't think Old or Middle English counts. If this experiment proves successful, I'll ask my polyglot friends to entertain the unicorns, too.'

'Good morning,' Adam said.

'Good morning. Oh, I already said that. Sorry.' Lily held the megaphone to her mouth and whispered, 'I'm just nervous. I really want this to work.'

'I do, too.' He took the megaphone and set it on the ground.

'So, you do care about curing cancer.'

'As long as Mathilda is happy.'

'That beautiful horse?'

'That was a disguise. Mathilda is a unicorn.'

Lily's eyes widened.

'How clever. I never would have guessed. Where is she now? And where's sweet Hazel? Wait. Is Hazel a unicorn, too? Is there such a thing as a donkey-corn because that would be adorable.'

'Hazel's a donkey, and they're both at the waterfall.'

'That's strange. I didn't see a waterfall on any of the maps.'

She followed Adam into the stable's tack room. It was windowless, dim, and smelled of leather. Bridles, halters, bits, and rope hung from pegs on the walls. Saddles, both plain and richly ornamented, sat on curved stands. He moved a peck of Cosmic Crisp apples aside to reveal a tiny blue door.

'Is that door for mice?' she asked.

'No, it's for us.'

'Well. Curiouser and curiouser. Do you have a potion for me to drink? I always wanted to walk through a forest of flowers and ride a squirrel through the trees.'

Adam pulled a key smaller than his pinky nail from his shirt pocket. He slid the key into a hidden notch in the wooden wall as he thought the password. The little door opened, and a band of pink light illuminated the room.

'Put your left foot in the door,' he said. 'Then be prepared for a falling sensation.'

'What happens if I put my right foot in the door?'

'Be prepared for battle.'

'Oh, I'm not ready for that. Left foot. Left foot.'

She slid her left foot into the doorway and disappeared. After securing the tack room, Adam grabbed the megaphone and four apples and followed her. After fifteen years as Mathilda's guardian, he still felt a thrill plunging down the flashing vortex. The second he emerged into daylight and his boots touched grass, he looked for Lily.

She'd fallen to her knees on the edge of a cliff, awestruck at the vista before her.

'This is splendid. Are we still on Earth?'

Unicorn Valley was on Earth, in a secret location only accessible through unicorn magic. It was basically Paradise – radiant clouds blushing pink and gold, lavender mountains trimmed with snow, green meadows, fragrant wildflowers. A shimmering waterfall, taller than the Eiffel Tower, splashed into a sapphire lake, creating misty rainbows.

Hazel trotted to Lily, braying her excitement.

'Hello, Hazel, sweetie. Did we bring apples?'

As Lily hugged the donkey and fed her an apple, Mathilda spoke to Adam.

I'm ready to make my big entrance.

Don't intimidate her.

You are so gone.

'Lily,' Adam said. 'I mean, Dr. Bly – '

'You may call me Lily,' she said softly.

Adam's breath caught, and he felt dizzy. No and no. He didn't need these distractions, not while trying to save poor, little, bald babies from cancer.

'Mathilda's here,' he muttered.

'Where?'

He pointed at the waterfall, and they both waited. For ten seconds.

You're such a drama queen, he thought.

Shut up. I'm magnificent.

Mathilda could assume many forms. Horse or unicorn. Large or small. But she was most comfortable in the form she'd taken during the Great Wars of Good and Evil during the Dark Ages. She emerged from the waterfall as a unicorn, horn first, as tall as a cathedral and emitting rays of blinding light. Her golden horn spiraled even higher, long as a cathedral's spire. It was stronger than any material known to man and could skewer three mountain trolls at once. That was not theoretical.

As Mathilda walked on the lake toward them, her glow reduced to mere angelic luminosity. Adam often sat on this cliffside to talk with her, face to face. He looked down at Lily who appeared spellbound. It was a common reaction to the opal glitter of the unicorn's coat and the iridescent, almost slow-motion flow of her mane and tail. The light of Mathilda's prismatic eyes on Lily's skin was enchanting.

'My vial isn't big enough.'

'This is your new vial,' Adam said, holding the megaphone, wide side up. He blocked the mouthpiece by shoving in three apples. 'I'll collect the tears.'

'Thank you.' Lily looked up at him, her face still rainbow-lit. 'I'm nervous.'

'You'll do fine. Mathilda has a silly sense of humor.'

'She does? Well, I can be silly.'

As Adam stepped back, Lily turned back to Mathilda, took a deep breath, and shouted, 'Absquatulate!'

The word echoed around the valley. Mathilda tilted her massive head but remained silent.

'Ballyhoo! Bloviate! Bum-fuzzle. Bung-hole!'

Mathilda snorted.

'Callipygian!' At that word, Lily wiggled her butt, and Adam felt feverish. 'Cattywampus! Collywobbles! Crapulence! Ding-us!' By now, a ridiculous pose or awkward kick accompanied every word. 'Diphthong! Dongle! Doohickey!'

At fartlek, Adam almost smiled. At flibbertigibbet, Mathilda tittered, a sound like thousands of windchimes sweetly ringing.

'Gazump!' Lily hopped, and a braid fell from its pins. 'Gongozzler! Gobbledygook! Hemisemidemiquaver! That's a 64th note. Hemi-semi-demi-quaver!'

Mathilda laughed, a sound like thousands of church bells ringing in jubilant harmony.

'Hoosegow! Hootenanny! Impignorate!'

Any minute now.

'Kerfuffle! Lollygag! Mollycoddle! Mugwump!'

Adam took a running leap off the cliff, holding the megaphone. He caught Mathilda's long, silky mane, one-handed, and swung back and forth a few times until he was in position to collect her tears.

'Nice jump! Nincompoop!'

Nice jump, Nincompoop! Mathilda howled. She laughed and pranced, her golden hooves kicking water. Large tears flowed from her eyes, silver and shiny as liquid mercury. Half of them splashed into the megaphone.

'Periwinkle! Pettifogger! Phalanges!' Lily turned a terrible cartwheel, and more braids tumbled loose. 'Piffle! Ragamuffin! Scalawag!'

By skedaddle, the megaphone was half full.

'Slumgullion! Snickersnee! Snollygoster!'

'It's full,' Adam shouted.

'I have to finish, or it'll drive me mad. Spleenwort! Taradiddle! Troglodyte! Whippersnapper! Whirligig! Wid-der-shins!'

Still laughing, Mathilda walked closer to the cliff. Adam stepped back onto land and gave the megaphone, brimming with cancer-curing unicorn tears, to Lily. She smiled up at him like he'd invented sunlight and ice cream. She was breathless, flushed, and gorgeous – a wild Pre-Raphaelite beauty, her braids unraveling. She'd lost her spectacles, and Adam saw amber flecks in her brown eyes. She smelled like vanilla and old books.

Beyond the physical, she was fearless of humiliation in pursuit of a noble goal. She was intelligent, kind to animals, a force for good in the universe, and she had an excellent vocabulary. He couldn't ignore his feelings any longer.

Unicorn Batman wanted to hug Dr. Lily Bly.

So, Mathilda said. *How does falling in love feel?*

Terrifying, he thought. *Wonderful.*

I believe she had you at 'callipygian'. That means having shapely buttocks.

Adam shook his head and smiled. She'd had him at *I need some unicorn tears.*

Square Lives

by Sarah Rigby

Highly Commended, Edinburgh Short Story Award 2025

Unless you live or work nearby you will not know this place. Apartment blocks and offices shield the central garden from sight. At night the square is quiet, streets empty, flats shut-eyed and the garden rests behind locked gates, observed only by an urban fox. But, in the daylight, its siren's call lures people in to walk and talk and contemplate in its breathing space.

At nine o'clock the man from the council unlocks the gates. Traffic crawls through the streets, its pollution filtered by the towering plane trees which edge the square, their peeling bark like camouflage. In summer their handspan leaves keep the city heat from the flats opposite, but now they are just skeletons, filigree against the cold white sky.

This is not a private garden, hidden behind a circlet of thorns, like Sleeping Beauty's bower, seclusion available to a selected few. No, this is a public park. The mower's nap is mirrored in the straight edged paths lined with sturdy benches. Lozenge-shaped flowerbeds make careful patterns, blocks of pink and yellow. But look out to the edges and the view is softened by the rampant growth of a dark leaved holly or feathery birch.

Soon after the gates open, Carys strides through them, propelling a stroller with jerky movements. It is only nine fifteen, but the grizzling teething child has driven her out of their confined flat. The space soothes. They stop to watch pigeons strutting at the foot of a bench, pecking at crumbs scattered by a wizened old woman muffled all in black. Her face is folded like a walnut shell. The child stops crying, sore cheeks numbed. He chuckles at their dipping heads and the way they swarm round each new handful of grain. He shouts as they take off en masse, when an old man and his grey muzzled Labrador approach. The man smiles at the young woman. One day he'd like to speak. He often sees her in their separate perambulations of the park.

Across the road at The Aubergine café Nnenna is on the morning coffee run. She usually volunteers so she can steal a few peaceful moments from the working day. It is not really robbing the company. She is often at work well before the others, getting everything ready for that day's mysteriously important meetings. Behind the counter Marcos gazes at Nnenna in admiration. She is tall with smooth brown skin, high cheekbones and large brown eyes. So far, he has dared do nothing but gaze. She does not seem to notice. She always has a slightly far- away look. Her eyes do not see the man who serves, the Marcos who loves Puccini and George Ezra, who in fact owns the Aubergine and longs to know her.

Nnenna watches a woman with a child in a pushchair. They are surrounded by pigeons, a bubbling sea at their feet. How lovely to be able to wander in the park whenever you want to, Nnenna thinks. Carys watches the birds with their constant flutter and twitter, hating them. They look dirty, but she tolerates them for Tom's sake.

Marcos has to call twice to attract Nenna's attention.

'Excuse me. Excuse me, your coffees are ready!'

'Sorry. I was miles away.'

Marcus laughed, 'I think you were doing as I do when the café is quiet.'

Nnenna frowns. What on earth is he on about? Does he mean skiving? Her conscience twinges.

Marcos falters, blushing.

'Watching the people in the park that is, making up lives for them'

This time Nnenna is the one to blush.

'Oh, yes,' she mumbles. 'I am afraid I do that. I always wonder what it's like to live a different life.'

'It's OK. I do it too, my customers, people in the park or on the tube. The old lady who feeds the birds every day, for example. I think she is the last descendant of a family of Russian émigrés who escaped the Revolution. She is very poor now but tries to keep up standards. She still has the family samovar, and each week invites her friends around and brews tea and serves little Russian cakes on a fancy cake stand, and wears her tiara, the last family heirloom which she cannot bring herself to sell, even though she has so little money, and no one to leave it to when she goes.'

Nnenna bursts out laughing. 'She's probably from Maida Vale, wouldn't know a samovar if it bit her and has never heard of the Russian Revolution!'

'I'm sure you're right. But perhaps…'

'I'd better take these coffees back before they get cold,' Nnenna says, but she is grinning..

'I hope to see you again soon.' Is that OK, Marcus worries, not creepy? Just friendly he hopes.

'I'm sure you will.'

Good. She has not been put off by his weird imaginings.

Nnenna notices how expressive the dark brown eyes with their long lashes are, how hopeful the face.

The door bangs open, and cold air eddies around Nnenna's legs as she turns to leave. Marcos' gaze breaks away from hers to greet the new customer. Business must go on. Although his hands are busy fulfilling their order Marcos sees Nnenna go.

'Take a seat, I will bring these over for you.'

'Thanks.' Carys smiles gratefully at him then steers Tom's buggy carefully between the tables to the one in the window. She undoes his straps and pulls him out onto her knee. Straight away she regrets this, as Tom feeling freedom, wriggles and struggles to get down on the floor, although he cannot yet do more than pull himself up. Carys takes the line of least resistance and lets Tom stand at her feet. He crows happily.

Marcos brings over her latte and cinnamon muffin, her treat. She shouldn't really. She still has plenty of baby fat to lose. It's a vicious cycle. She is fed up, stuck in the flat all day, feeling fat and unattractive and no longer Carys, so she eats to cheer herself up, but that doesn't help the weight and afterwards she feels worse. Still, she smiles at Marcos because he has a kind face, and lovely eyes, and isn't anything to do with babies. She hates the mother and baby groups. Loathes their iron-fisted competitive comparisons in the velvet glove of pseudo compassion.

The park is pulsing. A group of women with small children hogs the central pavilion. Now and again a small child darts out to be swiftly swept up by his carer, with the speed of a frog's tongue flicking flies. A fluorescent jogger, ponytail bouncing, runs diagonally across the middle, scattering pigeons. A small team of gardeners get to work. The man in charge watches two apprentices with little expectation. He's had a string of no-hopers recently. They think they want to garden, but then moan about the cold, about the physical work, about pretty much everything really. He begins to lay out the trays of winter bedding to keep going the succession of colour he prides himself on. This is the best part of his job. He offers to get coffees in first. Today's youth don't seem to be able to function without it. There's an excellent café across the square. Silly name, though, Aubergine.

Marcos greets him with his regulars' smile, warmer and wider than his automatic customer greeting.

'So, you are planting today?' he asks.

'Yes, my favourite. I'm hoping that the new lads are better than the last lot. Don't know much about plants yet, but they seem to get on with things.'

'And how is your wife?'

The laughter lines etched on Martin's ruddy face droop.

'Not good I'm afraid.'

'I am sorry.'

Martin nods. He'd like to say more but can't. Marcos wants to say something helpful, consoling, but what is there to say when someone is dying?

'Have a seat while I get these ready.' Back to business.

'Thanks.' Martin sits down next to Carys.

'Hello young man,' he says to Tom. Tom gazes up at him in fascination. 'You've got such rosy cheeks you could be a gardener like me.' Then to Carys, 'Teething?'

'Yes, unfortunately.'

'Not a good process, is it? Our granddaughter's going through it too.' He looks at Carys' face and sees the stress but can't think of anything helpful to say. His wife would know what to do. This is woman's work.

Carys thinks, 'What a kind face,' then Tom pulls the sugar bowl off the table. It smashes on the tiled floor; shards scatter and sugar cubes bounce under tables. Everyone looks. Carys shrivels. Who has sugar cubes these days Martin wonders.

Marcos hurries over with dustpan and brush.

'Don't worry, no problem,' he says over Carys' garbled apologies. 'Really, it doesn't matter,' when she offers to pay. Tom is wailing, frightened by the noise, until Martin picks him up and bounces him. The noise stops like a tap being turned off. Carys could hug this man, but his coffees are ready, and he goes back to the group of lads desultorily hoeing in the square. She straps Tom into his buggy and heads home. Maybe he will sleep after lunch.

Lunchtime is busy with office workers wanting sandwiches and twenty different versions of skinny soy latte double shot coffees. Smartly dressed staff pace the park's perimeter counting steps or huddle on benches to eat. After the rush, the afternoon is quiet, and Marcos has time to dream of Nnenna with the long legs and beautiful face. In her office across the road Nnenna too finds the afternoon drags. She thinks of Marcos' dark eyes and his lovely smile and decides to call in at the café on her way home, if it's still open.

Marcos closes early as he has had no customers since half past three. He runs automatically through his cleaning routine, coffee machine first, floor last, chairs upended on the tables. Just as he is putting out the rubbish, he sees Nnenna walk up to the main door. She has come. He dashes back inside to open the door for her. Marcos turns the sign to closed and rights two of the chairs near the bar.

Just as the gates are due to close, a man scurries in, laptop bag swinging. He is keen to get home to see his son Tom and crossing the park saves five minutes. He is surprised to see lights on in the café and the taste of coffee fills his mouth, but no, he'd better get home. Carys will be desperate. The Parks man locks the gate behind him and whistles back to his van, rubbing his hands to erase the touch of cold metal. The garden subsides gently as if exhaling a long-held breath.

In the café, Marcos and Nnenna no longer have eyes for the comings and goings of the square. Marcos has switched off the front lights, but the old woman watching from the kitchen of her tiny flat opposite, sees them in silhouette against the lit bar, dark heads leaning together. She cuts the crusts from a small pile of sandwiches and puts them aside for the pigeons. From a drawer she takes out a lace cloth and wafts it into the air to unfold. It flutters down on the table like the wings of white doves. Then she fills the gleaming silver samovar and places it in the centre and waits for the doorbell to ring.

Bhutto is Dead

by Saira Arian

Editor's Choice, Edinburgh Short Story Award 2025

The sun is sinking, and the air is stifling. I long for rest. The park is a sliver of shade in a relentless day. Children scream with excitement as they fly into the air on squeaky swings. I watch Nida playing on the slide.

I think of everything waiting for me at home. I should leave – so much to do. But Nida is happy. We hardly go out. Let her stay a little longer

The crowd thins. Thankfully, Nida gets a turn on the swing now.

'Look, I'm touching the sky!' she shouts with laughter.

'Yes.' I smile.

'Higher!'

'Higher!' she chants.

'Not too high,' I say. 'You could fall.'

'No, I won't fall. I can fly!' she calls.

I shake my head.

A group of well-dressed children gathers near the swing, their polished confidence unsettling. I pull Nida off.

'But I wasn't done yet,' she whines.

'It's enough,' I comfort her.

A little boy arrives, leading a small monkey by a rope tied around its neck. The monkey wears a fez hat.

'Walk like a gentleman,' he says. The monkey folds its hands behind its back and struts. Nida laughs.

'Fight like a mother-in-law,' the boy says. The monkey screeches, flailing its arms. Nida grabs my hand, her laughter faltering.

'Salute like a general,' the boy commands. The monkey stands straight, saluting sharply. Nida claps again, hesitant but entertained.

The well-dressed children laugh loudly and unapologetically but leave without paying. The boy scratches his matted head, his shoulders slumping. I untie the knot at the corner of my dupatta where I keep my money. I give Nida a twenty-rupee note. Shyly, she hands it to the boy, but the monkey grabs it and stuffs it under the boy's hat. Nida runs back to me, giggling.

The day is waning, but the heat clings stubbornly to the air. Light-headedness creeps in. 'Let's go home now,' I say.

'Just one more time on the swing, please.'

I swing her again, though my arms ache after the morning's cleaning jobs. Each push sends jolts of pain, but Nida is so happy. I let her smile carry me through.

A balloon man walks wearily toward us, holding colourful balloons. Nida jumps off the swing in excitement. She looks at me pleadingly, but I shake my head once again. She frowns and watches as the man twists and pinches a balloon into a dog. Then, oddly, he bursts it with a pin. The loud bang seems to freeze time. The park's noise recedes, and for a breath, the world is still. Absolutely quiet, like the beginning of time. Slowly the sounds rush back, louder than before, crashing over us like waves.

Smoke is rising from the far end of the park, dark and twisting into the evening air. The faint, acrid scent reaches me, mingling with the warm, spicy aromas wafting through the park. My stomach twists, hollow and raw. I haven't eaten since dawn – a watery cup of tea and a stale roti to keep me going. The ache deepens, the smells stirring a hunger I've grown used to ignoring.

The smoke lingers in my peripheral vision, an unsettling sense of dread twisting through me, as though dark threads dissolve into the sky.

Suddenly, the monkey darts out from the trees. The boy is nowhere to be seen. The monkey hands Nida her twenty-rupee note and makes a face – a mix of a smile and a grimace – before running back.

'Look, Maa!' Nida says, giving me the money. A wave of happiness washes over me, lightening my chest.

'God bless that monkey,' I whisper. I scoop Nida into my arms. For a moment, I feel unstoppable.

'Let's get a rickshaw,' I say. Her smile returns.

We walk past a corn cart, and my stomach growls.

'How much, bhai?' I ask the vendor.

'Ten rupees,' he replies.

'One bag, please,' I say. He cooks the kernels in hot sand, sifting them until they turn golden brown. I hand the cone to Nida, keeping just a few kernels for myself.

'All for me?' she asks, her eyes wide.

'Yes, my love,' I reply. 'Now let's get a rickshaw.'

The roads are chaotic, choked with traffic and pollution. Nida holds me tightly as I flag down a rickshaw. One finally pulls over. The driver nods at my address, and we climb in. The wooden seat is rough beneath me, but Nida drowsily curls into my lap, her small body light and warm. I smile, glad that she's had a good day.

The driver struggles through the jammed streets. Ambulances wail past.

'Why the rush?' I ask.

'Some rally,' he mutters, wiping sweat from his forehead.

The rickshaw pulls onto the pavement, jolting us forward. People shout at the driver, but he just honks and keeps going. Behind us, police begin blocking the road.

The driver turns on the radio. A song plays briefly, but then the broadcast cuts off.

'We are receiving information that Bhutto has been shot at her rally in Rawalpindi.'

I gasp, instinctively looking back at the park. The air grows heavier, and the day dims, as though the weight of the news had darkened the world.

Nida stirs in my arms, her small face pressing against my chest.

'Shh… shh… go back to sleep,' I whisper, stroking her hair. The rickshaw lurches forward, the sound of horns and sirens echoing around us.

All Not Breathing

by Ralph Bolland

Reader's Choice, Longlisted, Edinburgh Short Story Award 2025

Luckily this happened after the three sisters had got married so there wis only seven ay us on the back seat.

Dad was driving. Mum had a wean on her lap, and one settled in beside the handbrake. In the back there were four in a squishy row and us others were meant tae sit on laps, but usually we just scrunched up and packed doon aw ways. Before the weddings, two might be plonked on ginger crates in the footwells; maybe a wean on the parcel shelf. Once ye shut the doors it was fine.

So, we're all not breathing to get tae the end of the tunnel. That wis the game. It took aboot a minute to drive through. Dad would shout '*go*' and we'd aw play like maddies. Folk wid sometimes try to change the rules, like: '*Breathing-out's ok, but no breathing-in.*' Dad ruled that out cos it was sneaky.

He'd always remind us tae wave at the cameras. '*Gie the man a big smile!*' None of us had a scooby where the cameras wur. What kind of a job was checking cameras in the Clyde Tunnel, anyway?

'What's he looking for, Dad?' I asked.

'Leaks, maybe.'

'Leaks of water?'

'That's it. So we don't all die in a biblical flood.'

'Can there be leaks, but?'

'Aye. Ye mind the wee Dutch boy with his finger in the dyke?'

'We're under the water, Daniel,' said Elaine, next sister up. She'd listen for a pearl of Dad's wisdom then claim it as her own. 'Of course, there can be leaks.'

'Where is the water, but?' I asked.

'Above us,' said Dad.

'How do they make the tunnel?'

'They bore a big hole.'

'But the water would get in the hole.' Like at the seaside.

'They're not digging though the water. They're digging through the ground.'

'But where's the water while they're digging?'

'Above the ground.'

I didnae get that. But Dad was an Engineer.

There was a strict *'no farting'* rule in the car. Mum said it was *'too punishing for all'*. I once had the bright idea of farting during the game, while naebdy was breathing. So, twenty seconds in I had drilled out a quick percussion. Silent, of course, but you know straight-away if it's a toxic emission. Mum turned instantly to catch me scarlet-faced. I'd had nae time to blame anyone else.

'Who opened their handbag?' she asked.

Everyone was shaking their heads, glaring at me, some holding their noses. It was an awful lot of disappointment for one Peugeot. I complained that anyone who smelled it must be cheatin'. Dad chortled. Mum tutted.

Farting wasn't the problem this time. We'd gone to early mass: faces scrubbed and smart clothes on; the Big Peugeot was washed (we loved that motor) cos we were visiting a distant relative: an Irish priest who'd changed his name to the Gaelic and was staying in a seminary out by the middle of nowhere. Seminaries were where priests came from and this Uncle of ours knew the secret. Dad even told us he sometimes spoke in tongues and when we asked how that worked he jist said, och never mind.

Dad had turned off the Perry Como to let us concentrate on not breathing. There was daylight ahead on the rise out of the tunnel. People would start acting up in this last bit: waving hands, bigging up their eyes and spluttering. Shocking, it was. Dad swung the Peugeot out to where the exit slip roads were divvied up by huge, grey columns. Drew once told me these stanchions were what actually held the tunnel up. I didn't get it. He said it was hard to explain.

Out of nowhere the marauders swooped in a raggedy horde from either side of one stanchion. We all perked up like prairie dogs. Sunday morning's state-of-grace was quickly shot-to-buggery.

'Oh,' said Mum.

Traffic was light, but these guys poured right out onto the road. I straight away had an image of Campbells swooping down and slaughtering MacDonalds. But these guys had denim jackets and docs; Harringtons and bright Oxford bags; carrying bits of wood and other chibs. The leader had a stiff white crop of lavvy-brush hair and a red half-brick in his hand. Whoever they were looking for wasnae where they thought.

Driving through Glencoe once, Dad had told us the *'massacre'* story: scheming voices; screaming weans; blood and slaughter. Although it wisnae a western I'd always had an idea of the MacDonalds as honest, pioneer folks crossing an Oregon valley trail before the sly and blood-thirsty Campbells fell on them like an Apache war party. (I knew which clan was which cos the Campbells made soup out of the MacDonalds.)

Dad slowed the big Peugeot right down. Other cars drifted round and drove on. The bandits must have thought to look somewhere else and began to turn away, disappointed, trudging back up the grass embankment beyond the stanchions. Just as Dad began to inch the Peugeot forward a new face poked out from behind a column to our right. This guy wasn't looking, but hiding. His bug-eyes wheeled round quickly like a periscope. His chest was heaving. Was he having an asthma attack? Then he lurched off the grass and flung himself tae his knees on the road in front of us.

'My God,' said Mum.

Dad stopped the car. The guy clasped his hands before us then looked straight through the windscreen and mouthed *'please'*. He had nae jaiket on; his jeans and white shirt were mockit and he was crying.

The remnants of the gang – thirty yards away – had turned back to the roadway.

There. He. Is.

'Frightened for his life,' said Dad. 'Open the door, Drew.'

Drew – wedged up at the door wi Elizabeth and me – opened it too quickly and we all tumbled out on to the Clydeside Expressway. Drew managed tae get his feet planted on the road while me and Liz scrambled back into the car.

The gang were wired now but thinking in slow motion. Drew stepped away from the car and nodded to the open door, watching the guy. Mum watched Drew. Dad watched the maniacs. Once the penny dropped the guy took off along the tarmac like a dug who'd just been shown a sausage.

Dad's eyes were straight ahead. How long for the maddies tae reach us? Ten seconds? Five? Then Lavvy-Brush stepped back into view: *What's this shite?* He looked at us and roared something. Mum tutted.

'Come over in the front, Tony,' said Dad.

Tony, on Anne's lap to my left, leapt up to clamber through.

'Shift across back there,' said Dad over his shoulder.

Michael flew onto Anne's lap and we all budged up left. Drew stood aside and the guy barrelled into the car. Drew was almost in as Dad pulled away. It was like *'the Sweeney'*. The crying guy was on my lap. Lavvy Brush was running, screaming, yards away. Drew – squished against the door – was still on his feet when the half-brick crashed against the window and his backside. Dad swerved sharply but got an angry horn from behind and swung back again, flingin us all over the shop. Other motors picked their way round us and helped split up the gang as Dad got up tae speed and left Lavvy Brush hurling abuse in the rear-view mirror.

No-one was comfy. The big Peugeot was quiet and smelt suddenly rank. Although the guy was a state, he seemed more bewildered at how many folk wur piled into his getaway vehicle.

'Thank you, Mister,' he said, really quietly.

'That's alright, son,' said Dad.

No one spoke for a bit. I saw Dad check his mirror to look at the guy. He was snotty and shuddering, trying to catch himself. The back-seat cram hadn't sorted itself, but no one piped up. We were part of a heroic act even if the car was honking. Mum opened her window.

'Thank F-F-F...' the guy stuttered suddenly. 'Thank... fudge for that.'

Drew caught my eye. '*Fudge*'? But the poor guy was in a car with a big family, all dressed for serious chapel, who had maybe saved his life. Mum tutted anyway.

'Where d'you want to go, son?' asked Dad.

'Eh...' He didnae know.

'No rush. Take yer time.' Dad looked across at Mum and nodded.

The guy's shirt was soaking, plastered with wet dirt, grass and stuff. He had blood on his mouth and nose. He had ink-tattoos on three knuckles of his left hand.

'Drop me at Anniesland Cross, Mister?'

'Aye,' said Dad.

We drove on for a minute or so with just the stink and the noise of the guy snivelling. All of us not breathing.

'You'll be alright there?' asked Dad.

'Aye. Ah will be, Mister. Hanks.'

He took a big gulp. I wondered if he'd start crying again.

'Hanks a million, Mister. Saved my life.'

There it was. Official.

'You're welcome,' said Mum.

Then he did start crying.

None ay us said anything. None ay us moved. All getting nipped and squeezed and crushed a bit. Just embarrassed. Tryin to be grown-up but rattlin with how mental it was. I had a sneaky check down and saw his jeans all wet round the top of his legs. The knuckles of his left hand spelled: F. T. P.

'Thank Fudge,' he said.

Mum tutted again.

God Bless the Fried Chicken at Clucker's Sunday Lunch Buffet

by Holly Brandon

Reader's Choice, Longlisted, Edinburgh Short Story Award 2025

If the congregation of Charity Springs First Baptist Church was half as concerned with following Jesus as they were with the Sunday lunch buffet across the street, the good Lord would've yanked them up to Heaven like He did with Enoch. The buffet runs out of fried chicken every Sunday—usually within the first hour—and while it's not my place to judge, some of the things these folks have done to get their chicken fix are downright disgraceful.

I've seen families slip out during the benediction when they thought everyone's eyes were closed. I've seen others illegally park in handicap spots closest to the exit, bolting out of the chapel like cats on fire. Last week, Sandra Fields slipped my husband, Hank, a twenty to block highway traffic—he's the crossing guard—until her tacky convertible made it into the buffet parking lot. I have a front row seat to the chicken-induced chaos while our six boys and I wait for their father to finish his job.

'I'm hungry, Mom,' they whine. They're *always* hungry.

'Why's it taking so long for Dad to get back?'

As a thank you for Hank's superior cross-guarding, the owner of Clucker's lets our family eat for free every

Sunday after the traffic's cleared, but all that's ever left is sides and desserts. Hank is content with cornbread and black-eyed peas, while the boys fill up on macaroni and chocolate cake—which, I suppose, is alright once a week. Some mothers (I won't name names because I don't like to gossip) feed their children junk like that every single day.

'Mom, Peter's licking goldfish crumbs off the pews.'

'Mind your own business, Luke. I'm *starving*!'

I sigh and glance out the chapel window; traffic seems to be at a standstill. I grab my phone and call Hank.

He answers, out of breath. 'Hey honey, I'm trying to work h—'

'Hank, what on earth is going on out there? Why aren't those cars moving?'

Hank shouts over the grumble of impatient engines. 'Seems to be some holdup at Clucker's, and traffic's blocking the highway. Apparently they've got a sign on the door—hey!' Hank's voice grows distant as he shouts at someone. 'What's going on at the buffet?'

I strain my ears, but all I hear is muffled chatter before Hank's voice returns. 'Apparently, somebody stole the safe with the secret spices; the restaurant couldn't make their fried chicken today.'

I gasp. This is the most exciting thing to happen since the pastor's sister-in-law got caught using a store-bought pastry shell in the annual pie bake-off— though it still never stood a chance against my lemon meringue.

Clucker's famous fried chicken is widely considered the best in the state (though having never had the honor of tasting it, I can't speak to the validity of that claim, but judging by their lumpy mashed potatoes and under-seasoned okra, I have my doubts). Rumor has it the owner imports special spices from India and keeps them—along with his top secret recipe—locked in a fireproof safe under his desk.

'Don't you worry, Hank,' I say, rising from the pew. 'I'll figure out who took those spices.'

'Well I really wasn't all that worried ab—'

I end the call and turn to our boys. 'Time for a game of Sneaky Snakes.'

I've had to get creative in keeping these boys entertained on Sundays while we wait on their father. Things like reading, drawing, and Go Fish got old quick, so we started playing hide-and-seek. Luke came home one Sunday, recounting the scandalous story he'd overheard a church member whispering to another as he hid behind the pulpit.

Right then and there, I knew the Lord had blessed me with a gift, a way to know who amongst our congregation needed my heartfelt prayers the most. Thus, the game Sneaky Snakes was born.

'It's like hide-and-seek,' I'd told my boys, 'but *better.*'

In Sneaky Snakes, everyone is *It*, and everyone is seeking the same thing—information. Whoever gets the juiciest bit of intel wins bragging rights for the entire week.

'Matthew and Mark,' I say, turning to my eldest two, 'you boys cover the chapel.' They nod and shimmy underneath nearby pews.

'Luke,' I whisper, 'you and John take the bathrooms and hallways.' My middle sons hurry to their assigned locations.

Finally, I kneel down, face-level with our youngest two, the twins. 'Peter and Paul, I have a very important job for y'all. I need you boys to stake out the Pastor's office.' They nod simultaneously, wearing identical determined expressions. 'Oh, and see if y'all can sneak this basket of muffins onto his desk. He's been extra grumpy lately, but that's nothing your mama's cranberry orange muffins can't cure.'

They leave with the muffins, crouched and silent. I head back to the chapel, stopping short when I hear a hushed voice.

'… can't say I'm too upset about it,' someone whispers, a breathy giggle punctuating her words. I peek around the corner to find Millie Macintosh—owner of the town's only other lunch buffet, The Juke Box Grill—talking on the phone. 'We might finally be able to fill every table!'

The Juke Box is never full because no one wants to eat over-cooked catfish or soggy fries—at least, that's what I've heard other people say. I don't like to judge, but I suppose there's a reason that buffet's nicknamed The *Puke* Box Grill. They've been trying to get Clucker's famous fried chicken recipe for ages. I reckon the only reason they're still open is due to the jilted overflow from their competitors.

'I'll be there soon,' Millie says, walking towards the church exit, 'if I can get past all this traffic.'

Traffic you caused with your little spice heist, I think, watching her go.

'Mom!'

Matthew and Mark jog towards me, faces shining with triumph. 'We heard something *very* interesting.'

I shush the boys and usher them inside an empty classroom. I'd be devastated if someone misinterpreted our quest for justice as nothing more than idle gossip.

'Whatcha got?' I ask.

'One of Clucker's former waitresses was talking to her friend,' Mark explains.

'She was complaining,' Matthew added. 'She said she was tired of so-called Christians leaving big messes and shitty tips.'

'Don't say 'shitty,' baby.'

'Sorry, Mom. Just quoting.'

'I know, sweetie, it's not your fault some folks need a good mouth-scrubbing.' I give both of them a peck on the cheek. 'Good work, boys. Y'all go find your little brothers now, and bring them here.'

As Matthew and Mark obey my orders like the little disciples they are, I sort through the information we've gathered. I'd thought for sure Millie Macintosh and her garbage buffet was to blame, but now I'm wondering if Clucker's waitstaff had something to do with it.

While I'm pondering this, the classroom door opens and all six of my sons pour inside.

'Did my littlest snakes learn anything interesting in the Pastor's office?'

Peter shrugs. 'Not really.'

'The pastor didn't say much,' Paul said, 'but I put the muffins on his desk when he wasn't looking.'

I try to hide my disappointment before addressing Luke and John. 'Y'all hear anything good?'

John nods and Luke grins. 'Jason Ferngate,' they say in unison.

Of course. I should have guessed our church's loudest — and only — vegan member would be a prime suspect.

'What did he say?'

The boys explain how they overheard Jason's conversation in the men's restroom. He'd been overjoyed, blabbering on to anyone who'd listen about the number of chickens that would go uneaten today.

Paul's brows furrow. 'Doesn't he know those chickens are already dead?'

'Vegans aren't the smartest people since their brains are starved for protein.' I click my tongue and pat my twins on their matching heads. 'All we can do is pray for them; bless their hearts.'

My dress pocket buzzes with an incoming call from Hank.

'Hey honey,' I answer, 'we've got three possible –'

'Traffic's finally cleared. I'm walking back to the church now.'

'Well, did they find out who took the spices?'

'Don't know. I think everyone gave up and went to the Puke – I mean, the Juke Box Grill.'

'Oh! Speaking of – '

'Mom,' Mark's voice is hushed and urgent, 'the pastor is hauling something out to the dumpster.'

I hang up on my husband. He'll understand. This just got interesting.

I place a finger to my lips and signal for the boys to follow me. The pastor's eyes dart around the nearly empty parking lot as he hurries across it, a cardboard box in his hands – and I'd bet my best batch of biscuits he's got those spices in there.

The pastor. I should have known. That buffet's been a thorn in his side for ages. Folks are always ducking out of his services early, more worried about filling their bellies with chicken than filling their hearts with the gospel.

Matthew trips on a rock, sending it skittering across the pavement. The pastor halts, moving the box behind his back as he swerves in our direction.

I step forward, hand on my hip. 'What's in the box, Pastor?'

He gulps. 'It – I'm sorry. I didn't want anyone to find out. I just – '

'Just stole the fried chicken spices?' I ask. 'To stop folks from leaving early?'

'What? No, of course not. I – ' He sighs and lowers the box, revealing its contents. It's full of…

Are those muffins?

My muffins.

My mouth falls open, and I raise my eyes to his.

'I'm sorry,' he says, scratching his neck. 'I didn't want to hurt your feelings, but these things are tougher than shoe leather. I've been using them for doorstops so they wouldn't go to waste, but a man only needs so many doorstops.'

While I'm trying to process this, Hank pulls up in our minivan. 'Hey there, Pastor.' He turns to me. 'Hey, honey. You and the boys ready to eat?'

The kids cheer their reply and leap into the van. I'm still staring at the box of muffins when Paul shouts, 'Hey, what's this?'

The pastor and I turn to see Hank jerk the driver's door open, jogging to the back of the van where the twins have climbed into the cargo area.

'What's this?' Paul repeats. He's pointing at a heavy black box with a combination lock at its hinges and a large yellow sticker that reads 'Top Secret.'

Hank turns cranberry red, eyes flitting between the box, the pastor, and myself.

'Hank,' I whisper, 'please tell me that's not – '

'I couldn't take it another week!' Hank wails, burying his head in his hands. 'Y'all don't know what it's like, watching everyone come out of there all happy and full, knowing you'll never taste that famous fried chicken that puts those smiles on their faces.'

'But Hank,' I whisper, placing a hand on his arm. 'Why on earth did you steal the spices?'

'I didn't *steal* them. I just *hid* them.' He wipes his face on the back of his sleeve. 'I was gonna bring them back, say I'd found them out in the ditch or something. I was hoping they'd fry up some chicken for us as a thank you maybe...' He trails off, staring at his feet.

I squeeze his arm, but the pastor speaks first. 'There is no man among us who is without sin,' he says kindly. 'And to tell you the truth, I wouldn't mind a piece of that chicken myself.' The pastor clears his throat, then says, 'I'd be happy to keep what I heard and saw to myself, if your family's willing to extend me the same courtesy – and maybe pay me a little favor?'

When the next Sunday came, my Sneaky Snakes had a brand new mission: to slither down the aisles at the end of the pastor's sermons, securing the exits with muffin-shaped doorstops.

From that day forward, not a single piece of fried chicken touched a church member's plate until the pastor's last word had been spoken.

Amen.

Fermenting

by Kája Kubičková

Reader's Choice, Longlisted, Edinburgh Short Story Award 2025

I started to ferment in November.

I threw myself into it with the kind of burning obsession generally reserved for sports fanatics and boy-band listeners. My afternoons were filled with lovingly doting over scobies, cooing over the bubbles they exhaled into kombucha mixtures. I cut up fruit, experimented with tinned peaches, fresh berries, passionfruit, pomegranate, mint. My flat began to look like an alchemist's laboratory: flasks with slowly fizzling liquid and circular floating scobies, jars with cut-up vegetables simmering in bubbling fluids, strangely smelling dough puffing up in containers and me, hunched over a recipe book muttering about batches and ratios and timings. My flatmate found it quietly disturbing. I would have expected more understanding from him, an art student. He was going through a phase of trying to work with 'mobile media', where he would fill up the bathtub, pour tinctures into the water and then take black-and-white photographs of his rippling face. I thought it must be terrible for the psyche, looking at one's distorted reflection like that for hours on end, though I never said that.

He hardly ever cooked, preferring to subsist on emphatically brown take-out: sad, limpid fries, dollops of thick gravy, and all that resting on a bed of hard rice and fried chicken. I made him a jar of kimchi, bright red and tied up with twine. I brought it over, knocked on the bathroom door. He made a noncommittal sound which I took to mean 'Please, come in!' and so I did. He was kneeling by an empty bathtub, his eyes fixed on the drain.

'Hi.'

'Hello.' He didn't look up at me.

'I made you kimchi.' He shifted.

'That's kind of you.'

'Yes. I'd say so.' I stood there, awkwardly cradling the kimchi in my upturned palms. I shuffled closer to him. Knelt on the ground. Put the kimchi by his feet. 'Is this a new piece?'

'No.' He shook his head. 'This is a bathtub.'

'Oh.' Pause. 'Well, I'll leave you to it.'

We were never close, but I thought that the fermenting might fix that somewhat, that if I let myself be bizarre as well, we could rejoice in being bizarre together. I talked to him about probiotics, showed him my scoby – the thick, jelly-like substance of bacteria and yeast that fed and nourished my drinks. He touched it with a knobbly finger and recoiled.

'That thing's *alive?*' he asked, bemused, disgusted.

'Sure!' I said helpfully. 'It's really less one thing and more millions and millions of little things.' I threw him a big smile. My braces had just been tightened, and even the small movement made my cheeks ache. 'You can even eat the scoby itself!'

He wrinkled his nose. 'No thanks.'

I cradled the scoby to my chest.

Leah sat on my bed, smoking.

'You really shouldn't smoke here.' I pointed out. Leah blew smoke out the window, leaned over and kissed me on the cheek. Her breath smelled of cigarettes and faintly of milk.

'I'm sorry, love, I'm sorry. I'm just so *stressed*.'

'About the-'

'About the gig, yeah.' Leah exhaled. She was trying to make it as a DJ at the moment, less so because of a passion for music and more because her ex-girlfriend had tried and failed to do the exact same thing. My friend was motivated primarily by a desire to prove herself to people she no longer loved. It was a trait which she seemed to display proudly: *look, here is how I'm fucked up. I know it. I embrace it. I'm happy anyway.* I was both in love with and envious of this self-confidence. I thought it must be nice, to know yourself so well that you can turn your maladaptive idiosyncrasies into goals.

'You'll be amazing.'

'Yeah, I will. I'm still nervous.' Leah took a mug off my dresser (my toucan mug, with a long orange beak and big sad bird eyes, my favourite) and dropped the cigarette in it. 'Can I kiss you?'

I cocked my head. 'Are you upset?'

'No.' Leah huffed, lay back on my bed. Her bangs had almost grown to cover her eyes, big and sad and calf-like. 'I'm over femmes. I'm over women. I've decided I only want to date quirky nonbinary people that are called, like, fucking, Tree, or Soup, or something. And I want to live in a cottage and make my own jewellery line with them and we'll probably have a big dog and no kids.'

'You're allergic to dogs.'

'Okay. A cat.'

'I'm not a quirky nonbinary person. Or called Tree. Or Soup.'

'Right.'

'I'm just me. Sorry to disappoint.'

'Well, you're queer. You're quirky. What, you haven't thought about it? You must have.' She ran a hand down my forearm. Her nails were bitten down to the meat. I caught it, circled my thumb over the fine bones of her fingers.

"Would you like some sourdough?"

In the kitchen:

Jars of preserved fruit, screwed on latticed tops.

Sourdough starter, lovingly parented.

Kimchi happily squatting in the fridge.

A pot of homemade yogurt curdling.

And my baby kombucha, gurgling away.

I thought of them while walking to class, when dancing with my friends. In my lectures, I wrote quick recipes in the margins of my notes. Leah came over to help me chop and jar and taste sometimes. She said she liked this on me, this feverish obsession. I wondered whether she said that because she loved me or because the artist in her revelled in the weird and the obscene, and decided that it ultimately didn't matter.

She asked what I liked about it and what I liked was everything, but what I said was:

the post-human, the

symbiotic colonies of creatures creating a unified whole,

giving and taking,

changing,

the way i would never want to be pregnant and exist to give my body over to something else but maybe i'm a hypocrite for finding it abhorrent because i want to house and nurse these little creatures and maybe i just hate to do what my mother told me to do and
the way i was taught to think of food not with love but with fear, the way this is changing and is changing me, too, and i like to think i do not exist alone in this change but with them and perhaps
i can noncommittally nurture rather than just consume.

January.

It was a new year and I was back from a dreary holiday in

my family's town. My sourdough starter had died over Christmas break.

Leah and I took it out of the glass bowl and placed it under the rotting cherry tree in my garden, dug a hole with our bare hands and placed it softly into the earth. Then we sat in the warmth of my kitchen, picking out dirt from underneath our fingernails. My flatmate wasn't yet back from a trip to Chile photographing a tree fungus.

I told Leah I was worrying about graduating. She laughed.

'Yeah, love. I hate the idea of endings. That's what a PhD is for.' She was in her first year of studying representations of gender in Slavic literature, focusing on Milan Kundera.

'I don't want a PhD.'

'Of course you don't. You're cut out for something different.' She flipped through a copy of *The Joke*. She hated that book, always kept it in her handbag.

'What am I cut out for?'

Leah looked at me, shrugging. 'Something different.'

She'd read *The Joke* seventeen times.

'But *what?* It's like everyone *knows*, like everyone has some kind of burning passion or a reason to keep existing, love, hatred, even strong ambivalence! And all I've got is… a bunch of dead sourdough.'

Leah snuggled up closer to me. We were on the couch watching a terrible reality TV show and eating burned popcorn. Her heavy body draped over me, usually so comforting, felt suddenly claustrophobic.

'I'm just scared,' I said in a small voice. Her cold hand on my forehead, a dead woman's hand, her hair stringy, straw.

'Me too.'

Instead of spending time on my thesis, I began to construct the glass jar.

It took a lot of ingenuity. It had to be made with a good system of vents, solid airflow, and a wide enough base that I could comfortably lie down and sleep. I'd considered learning to sleep standing up, but a quick Google search proved it would likely be too difficult for someone already predisposed to insomnia.

Then, the matter of the yeast and bacteria.

I wasn't a student of either medicine or biology, and I didn't want to worry any friends by asking. Armed with a formidable stack of books on human physiology, bacteriology and mycology, I holed myself up in the library.

For the first time in a while, I was excited. I had a *plan*. I fended off Leah's invitations to go to open mic poetry nights, potlucks and walks and coffee breaks. I understood, for the first time in my life, what it was to be a one-track-person. I thought this must be what having a child feels like – this sudden shift in perspective, a moment of clarity, sleeplessness, wondering whether this is joy or something closer to insanity.

It was nearly finished when my flatmate got back from Chile. He'd plaited his hair and wore baggy pants made from threaded-together bags of flour. He walked into the living room and found the glass jar, nearly two heads taller than me, thick, beautiful and grotesque. It was surrounded by smaller jars of various fermenting vegetables in a scene reminiscent of the ritualistic. He only looked at me, cocked his head.

'Are you still fermenting?'

'I've only just begun.'

He stared at the glass jar for a moment silently. Then, he nodded. 'Good. I think it's nice that you've found a passion.' He walked away, and all I heard was the sound of running water as he began to fill up the tub. It was so soothing of a sound I could have cried.

I had to eventually ask Leah to help me.

After nearly three weeks of little to no contact, she appeared at my door when I'd called, nonplussed, holding an order of chips in one hand and a bottle of orange juice (without pulp) in the other, what I called my favourite everything-and-anything remedy. I took her to the jar. I walked her through the bacteria I'd obtained, the yeast I'd bought. She frowned, absentmindedly eating a few of the chips she'd brought.

'And you're sure this is what you want?'

'Definitely.'

'Okay.' She put her bag down, rolled up her sleeves. 'Do you have a dolly, maybe? Anything with wheels. And some rope.'

'I love you, Leah.'

'I know, babe. Let's get you to where you belong.'

We moved it in the middle of the night. The roads were emptier, so we could maneuver the contraption through the city smoothly. We'd ended up tying the jar to my flatmate's longboard – the whole thing shook precariously over the cobblestones and potholes, but it held surprisingly steady. After three hours of arduous manual labour, Leah alternating between giggling at the situation and half-heartedly cursing me out for making her exercise, we arrived on top of Calton Hill. We untied the ropes, shuffled the jar down, and I took my pots of bacteria and yeast out of my backpack.

Finally.

In the morning, the dog-walkers would likely find me first, before the eager tourists could come with their cameras and cellphones. A new Edinburgh staple: the Fermenting Woman.

Submerged in a stew of bacteria, of yeast, bathing, nude, more-than and less-than. Part of a whole. I give myself over, my body, soul, mind. I exist to be viewed, to be changed, to be consumed.

Inside the glass jar, like a strange, pale fish, you can see me on sunny mornings, swimming, swimming, smiling, and fermenting.

Locusts and Dragons

by Genevieve Flintham

Reader's Choice, Longlisted, Edinburgh Short Story Award 2025

It descended from late summer. You licked a watermelon ice lolly n told me that dragons weren't real. I gnawed on a hunk of dirt n called you a liar. The pink melted n overtook your hand.

Your parents had a freezer out back. They weren't worried about electrical storms – not like paw, who refused to keep electrics.

That month, locusts overtook the sky. The neighbours said it was because someone's paw was summit bad. We didn't know what summit bad meant, but we liked to watch the locusts make shapes. We weren't scared.

You taught me how to make fire. I watched your stubby fingers – you rubbed two pieces of wood together, waitin' for the burn. It didn't come, but I knew what to do in case of emergency. That's what you said – in case of mer-gency. I laughed, cos you sounded like Officer Dan, who everyone laughed at.

Officer Dan hated the locusts. What kinda Officer is *scared of the damn bugs*, Paw said – a lot. He hacked a laugh and a lick of spit down to the floor anytime he spoke. I learned how to dance cross the wet patches. It was sort of a game. *What kinda kid needs a damn school*, Paw would say, like he was saying *what kinda kid needs damn rabies?*

It got weird, cos the locusts were just hovering toppa Paw's plot. They dint go near your house, even though you had the food n your parents knew how to build fire n they had BBQs in the backyard, grilling a hunka whatever Murphys Meat had goin'. Even though we could all see the smoke climbin' from your maw n paw's house – like a huge hand saying *look at me, I'm rich* – the locusts dint see it.

It was real nice of you to bring me leftovers, even though it grabbed the black eyed locusts. Thas when they'd swoop down, as if they were punishing me for stealin'. The bugs made real nice dragon shapes though, so I dint mind sharin'. The sound of their wings was like a song; I hummed along as I shoved my hands up in the air, holdin' the meat rind like some kinda offering.

You called me loopy, but thas only cos your parents said it. I know because I heard through your back window when Paw had the world locked out. I sat outside n heard you all talkin' – boring things like the weather n who was gonna elect themselves for summin – n then they talked about the loopy girl next door n said they dint want their boy hangin' with her no more.

I liked that they said 'loopy' – it sounded like the shapes the locusts made when they were entertainin' me. I heard your maw say that my paw had brought the dratted plague. You said village gossip was conjecture. Your paw was mighty proud of you using a long word, and that was that.

Conjecture. I liked it too. I sang it as I danced, waiting for the locusts to do summit. But they ignored me, mostly, less I had food. I sank into the ground a bit, because humans gotta eat too. Sometimes an eagle would come through the sky and scare them away. Once, I saw them crowd round our metal chimney pot like they wanted to climb down. But the chimney's got a hat on – prolly to stop the rain – so they all just blowed there like a balloon on toppa Paw's roof.

Officer Dan gave up on the *damn bugs*. When they were on the town it was everyone's prolem, but after they moved to our plot, no one cared. You said the bus genalman changed route, so no one had to see the clouds down our road. Your parents were worried their house was worth less now, but I told you that it would be worth *more*, cos the locusts created *silence*. No one could see your house past mine – no one on the bus was watchin' us by then.

Paw's house kept changin'. Sometimes it changed five times in one day – but thas just my 'magination, I guess. Sometimes nails n sometimes smooth, sometimes crackin' n sometimes pursed together like your maw's porch screen. I blinked n Paw's house changed, a hundred years old, then one, then some kinda relic. Just like me – sometimes I blinked n I wasn't there no more – sometimes I blinked n I was a superhero, a pirate.

We was the Universe I guess, always changin', diff-rent from one blink to the nother. *Nothin' is certain,* thas what Paw used to say, after maw sank. I repeated it a lot, like the chug of a hungry train: nothiniscertain, nothiniscertain, huff!

Loada rubbish though cos I knew you was gonna get A in numbers, n you did – showed me a scratchy chicken mark last time I saw you for real. That was certain –

could've told your maw she dint need to cry. Could've told your paw he dint need to look at me like I might steal the chicken mark – still wet from the teachers pen, looked like – right off the *damn* page.

Sometimes, I tried to catch a locust to eat. But they were too quick – *all the damn time*, as my paw might've said. Even if I rolled in the mud bog, even then they saw me comin'. Quick as a streak of muck-red lightnin', I'd leap into the air, but they'd be gone.

Officer Dan dint have a warrant. I felt bad for 'im, never havin' one. Paw said *warrant* like *Christmas present*, summit that Dan should really have, as Officer. But Paw also said it like he'd just eaten a roast duck, licking a hunk of spit down to the half floorboards as he choked n laughed.

Paw should be Officer really – he's always got one ear on the wind. Even when Dan *did* get a warrant – n I was real happy for him – I said congratulations when he showed up – he dint find what he was lookin' for.

The shack, the hut, the recycled altar from the church what burned down. A waste of space, Officer Dan grunted, as his colleague muttered the altar bit under his breath, one big hiss: aramshacklewasteofrecycledaltarwood.

Rodents n draughts n empty bottles what clank too loud n floorboards what moan n a demented armchair n a lifetime of *shitting inanity* – he listed it under his breath. No maw though.

Next day, when Dan left us alone, the locusts sang. Big song it was – caught my ears n wouldn't let go. They moved, so I followed n we all drifted as one n I felt like a fallen angel being dragged by black balloons.

Some kinda mallard ducks had got confused n taken a home out back of Paw's house, chewin' on the ground like they'd started eatin' ants. Where the bog met the changin' wall – nail brick, smooth oak, crumblin'– the birds tried ta sing, but nothin's louder than them locusts.

Could've prolly drawn them, if I had anythin' more than mud – n I was lucky cos there were three colours that fall. The red stuff nearly stained me – I was pretty sure I'd marks round my wrists, like I'd been dragged by Paw and not by the growlin' of my stomach, howlin' like a beast.

Their wings beat. They made me think of a tune that went *hot holly cold holly hot holly* as they dragged me long – tune was made up, but it matched their tug or the slug of my toes in the dirt. Not real toes, course, but it was hard to tell where they stopped n I started by then. hand.

You'd put an ice lolly stick on the grave what Paw had dug. You kept his secret, I guess. Prolly you were glad you didn't get heat from your maw no more, tellin' you not to hang out with Loopy. Can't hang out with a corpse.

Cute that you left the lolly there, remind me o' good times. You used to gimme the stick to suck n I'd chew it raw til it turned to splinters n embedded shards of melon – still there like a hinta sucked dry tobacco – in the top of my gob. I'd never tasted anythin' so good, n I'd stolen Paw's old spice from the floorboards enough.

That was before your paw decided lollies were sugar n before you told me dragons dint exist. That was before the ground chewed and the locusts came and the skin on my stomach ripped off and made little shadow puppets of beasts what danced across my ribs singin' *hot holly cold holly.*

I dint stay, even though the locusts were actin' like I shoulda stayed all day and done summin. Like what, prayed? Prayed at my own grave, can you imagine? Well, *you* couldn't ever imagine, cos you don't have any 'magination.

Neeway.

I told you to take the chimney top off. Whispered it to you when you was sleepin', so you wouldn't be freaked out. You musta thought you dreamed that loopy dead girl was talkin' loopy again.

But you did it. Next day, cranking off the chimney with a squelchy pop. Big job for a kid, but thing'd become rust. You was a little gargoyle for a minute there, all frozen with one expression in your empty cheeks – lookin' round like you thought you was on top of a church.

Light kept you safe n showed you the tiles – or what was left of them neeway – n it was like watchin' some heraldic beast dissect themselves from top of St Andrews Church. You looked mighty handsome even as you looked ugly, like everythin' that's beautiful is hideous too.

That's when they started loopin' properly. Great swarms creatin' shapes in the air, like one huge dragon. You got out the way just in time, shimmying the tiles like the light'd told you where to go.

Took less than one minute I'd say for them to swoop down the chimney, bout a million locusts n just Paw's hut. The walls changed again n I blinked n then one fell down. Prolly took another minute for them to split him apart, skin from splintered bone, or thas what it looked like.

I dint want God to kill him – or the universe or the locusts or whatever they was – I just wanted them to take him apart for a minute. Chew him up, curse him summit awful, pound him into spit n splatter 'im on the floor, fore puttin' him back together.

But they killed him alright, cos God is unforgivin', I guess, or because He really loved me, or summin. I like to think the last one, that maybe He was some angry big brother gettin' all 'gressive down the chimney n punishin' Paw.

You saw the dragon reappear, n I saw you smile. Proof that dragons were real. You lifted your hands to make a frame with your fingers n clicked, like you was takin' a mental photo. The air was red for a minute – blood I guess, or dragon's flames.

You took the photograph with you, n I knew you'd done your time, like a gargoyle what's fallen off in a storm. You'd left the church n you wasn't gonna look back, not when your maw was so proud at you gettin' the grades, n your paw liked you to say 'conjecture' over grits in the backyard.

First, I was angry that you never looked, but then I thought maybe that was the trade – He killed Paw for lettin' me star-ve, but He also stole you to somewhere better.

After that, the locusts disappeared. Which was a shame, because the bus genalman came back n all them people passed again, gawpin' at the shack like they was afraid of it, specially when Officer Dan found me.

After that, your parents talked about their house price *all the damn time.*

Chicken Bones

by Katy Walker

Reader's Choice, Longlisted, Edinburgh Short Story Award 2025

The fabric is cheap, almost weightless. It reminds Johnny of the Fuzzy Felt boxes he'd had as a kid – stick the farm animals in their pens, or the families safely in their houses.

It takes him a while to work out which way round they go – whether the decorative panel goes at the front or the back. Front, he decides, faintly repulsed by the small rectangle of gaudy, red and yellow flowers. They're slightly off-centre, as though the factory worker in… (Johnny checks the label) Cambodia has nothing but disdain for whoever's buying this crap. And no wonder – he is going to look such a tit.

It comes with a shirt as well, 100% polyester, but Johnny draws the line at that – one stray spark and he'll be ablaze like Guy Fawkes. But he's not going to think about things like that. He takes a blue checked shirt from the drawer and adds it to his overnight bag. Lays the budget lederhosen on top. Lets his hands rest on the barely-there softness of them. Wills himself to lighten. 'Right,' he says, closing the bag and heaving it off the bed. 'Let's do this.'

If there's one thing you can't postpone it's your own child's birthday, regardless of what else is going on in the world. He'd felt bad for asking but his producer had said they'd manage. Later she'd shoved an envelope into his hand, scrawled with Raff's name. 'Tell him to spend it unwisely,' she'd said. 'And give him a hug from me, will you, if he'll let you?' She'd known Raff since he was a toddler and, if things had been normal, she'd have been invited too. Johnny had felt suddenly emotional.

'Sure,' he'd managed, busying himself with folding the envelope and tucking it into the breast pocket of his flak jacket. 'Thanks.' He couldn't risk catching her eye.

A moment, and they were back to the usual banter. How *she* should be thanking *him*, for the opportunity to switch things up a bit. Give viewers a break from the middle-aged white guy. Give the newbie, Katia, a chance to prove herself. Johnny's face must have given him away because she added, smiling, 'Or not.' Johnny, to his slight shame, had instantly hoped for the latter – despite everything, he wasn't done yet.

As he parks his bag in the hallway now, less than eight hours later, he is struck by a fleeting, unfamiliar feeling. What is it? Doubt? Shrugging it off, he checks his phone again for the channel's live feed. Nothing yet, which Johnny can't decide is a good or a bad sign.

'Are you driving or am I?' he asks, coming into the kitchen. Beth is attaching a pair of artificial plaits to her head and speaks through a mouthful of hairpins. 'I don't mind. You probably need a few, don't you?'

'Depends. I'm not spending the whole night drinking pissy lager out of a plastic cup.'

'Ah.' Beth takes the pins out of her mouth. 'I admire your optimism,' she says, and turns to face him, plaits attached if somewhat precariously. Before she can say anything else, Johnny picks up the car keys from the bowl on the counter and dangles them between them. 'What's the German for 'Let's go'?'

'What's the German for anything?' Beth counters. 'What's the German for 'We could have been having a nice meal at The Ivy?'

The Sat Nav takes them off the A3 to avoid congestion and Johnny busies himself checking the suggested route. Raff rings to tell them he's managed to get them a room at the venue after all so they no longer have to slum it with The Youth at the Airb'n'b, and they won't have to drive either. It's a suite, he tells them, incredulous, his voice crackling through the car speakers. Same price as a double, Dad, don't worry. He's just seen it, he says, laughing – it's massive, with a marble bidet and a view of the bins. Beth thanks him for considering his aged parents' every need.

'How's Dad?' The question hangs in the air between Johnny and Beth. They made it a rule, years ago, not to talk about Johnny's job, and Raff has never really shown an interest. He wonders what Raff knows. Wonders if he's going to have to have a serious conversation.

'The usual,' Beth says, saving him. 'Tired and grumpy. Doesn't want to spend all night drinking pissy beer out of a plastic cup – do you darling?'

'That's not what I…'

'Dunno why not,' Raff laughs, as the notifications start to come through on Johnny's phone. He reaches instinctively for his breast pocket, but Beth gives him a quick, sharp glance and he stops, lifting both hands in exaggerated apology.

'Oh yeah, and guess what, Dad?' Raff continues. 'For a tenner you can get your very own souvenir tankard.'

Johnny forces himself to concentrate on his son. His stupid, gorgeous son.

'Wow,' he says. 'What's the German for whoop de fucking do?'

There is indeed, as promised, a view of the bins, complemented by the singularly incongruous blare of the oompah band, which blasts from the function room every time someone comes out of the fire escape for a smoke, or a snog, or a piss. Johnny stands at the window watching, while he waits for Beth to re-attach her plaits, which have fallen off again. 'Come up with me,' she'd said, and he was pleased to have an excuse to escape. It occurs to him now, as he leans his forehead on the window glass, that perhaps she'd been issuing an invitation. Is that what he needs, he wonders? To bury himself in her? Or is that... disrespectful? Twelve hours since he left. Less than twenty since he was staring down a different alleyway. Below him now, round the back of a small businessman's hotel on the outskirts of Bristol, where his son has unaccountably chosen to celebrate his twenty-first birthday at an event that seems to Johnny not dissimilar to a Hieronymus Bosch painting of hell, someone rounds the corner. Johnny freezes. The figure, dressed in kitchen whites, dumps a couple of bin bags on the ground and disappears back around the corner. Johnny's ears fill with sirens and screaming and he's in that other alleyway, willing himself to turn round, go back, to un-see.

A flash of colour drags him back. A fox. He says it out loud. Say what you see, wasn't that it? He vaguely remembered it from the last time, after Texas. They were entitled to six sessions. Encouraged, so long as it was in your own time. Johnny had put it off, hoping he'd fall off the list like he had all the other times, but the therapist had tracked him down, pestered him until he'd given in. 'A fox,' he says again, feeling his chest tighten and the breath squeeze up into his mouth. 'A fox. A fire door. A bin.' His mind flits to Katia and what she's seeing now. How she'll cope. He presses his head harder into the glass – then he realises what the fox is going to do. 'Fox'. Black plastic. 'Fox.' Tearing it open.

'Don't!' he shouts at the fox, as Beth appears from the bathroom. She lays her hands gently on his shoulders and pushes them down.

'It's okay,' she says. Johnny forces himself to keep looking. The fire doors open and a shaft of light drives the fox away, leaving the contents of the bin bag strewn across the alleyway.

'You can stay up here if you want. He won't notice. They're all plastered.'

Johnny swallows, forcing the bile back down.

'Nein,' he says, adopting a deliberately crap accent. 'Ve shall not be defeated! Vunce more into ze breech, dear friends!'

Beth follows him out of the room.

'I don't remember Shakespeare being German. Or Churchill. If that's who you were being…'

The oompah band has cranked it up a few notches, pausing every now and then so that people can shout 'Eins, Zwei, Drei' and down their drinks. Raff and his mates are on the dance floor, sweating a 50/50 mix of alcohol and life. Beth has gone to the Ladies to share her tips on reattaching fake plaits. The music stops and the people follow their cue: 'Eins! Zwei! Drei!' Johnny drinks, hoping to drown the bobbing images. An alleyway. Black plastic. Desperate hands tearing.

Raff is there, hand out, dragging him to the dance floor. He goes, taking with him an image of the Maenads on Mount Olympus, dancing and dancing themselves into a state of ecstasy, of leaving their own bodies behind. He dances, to celebrate his son's birthday. He dances, because tomorrow he must get on a plane and fly back to a war zone. He dances, to stay in this ridiculous, glorious moment, where young people can laugh and dance and live, and where bin bags contain only chicken bones.

In a Nutshell

by Andrew Burnet

Reader's Choice, Longlisted, Edinburgh Short Story Award 2025

I

The walnut sat alone at the centre of the table, cocooned in its shell. It was the last walnut, and both of them knew it. They sat there opposite each other, contemplating the nut.

Their hair was grey and thin. Their faces were lined. His cheeks were pink and rounded; hers were pallid and gaunt. They had been together many years.

They were in the kitchen of the house they had occupied for most of their marriage. The table was solid oak, marked by dozens of forgotten scores and stains. It was bare, aside from the walnut and the nutcrackers. A clock ticked in the corner.

He sighed deeply. 'I can't believe they've let – '

'Don't,' she said, calmly, firmly. 'Don't.' She placed a soothing hand on his, and felt it relax.

He looked up into her grey eyes and nodded. She nodded too.

II

The walnut's shell was hard but wrinkled. He thought of a partly deflated football. She thought of his scrotum, clenched tight on a cold day, and let out a low chuckle.

'What?' he said, surprised and curious.

'Nothing,' she said, playful and reassuring.

He eyed her quizzically, then returned his focus to the walnut. He picked it up, gently, between thumb and middle finger, and held it between them. Equidistant; sharing.

Its shell was formed from two bonded, dimpled halves. She ran a finger lightly along the seam that ran around it where the halves met. She thought of careful stitching. He imagined welding.

Inside, he thought, the flesh was formed from two convoluted lobes, hard but yielding.

She pictured the kernel, swelling with life as it grew inside its shell.

III

The kitchen was a warm, bright, lived-in space. It was the focal point of their home. They had spent countless hours sitting here, chatting, cooking, drinking tea, reading, playing cards, eating, watching television, welcoming friends and family.

The window framed a view of their little garden, the walnut tree, the landscape beyond. So many times, they had watched in awed silence as the dying sun robed these hills in luscious pinks, opulent yellows, livid purples.

Around the stove, a clutter of ageing photographs offered momentary glimpses of other views, other faces, other possibilities. A world far beyond their little cell. A host of possible avenues that they once explored, or might have explored. But as time had scoured away their youthful vigour, their inclination to venture beyond these safe, familiar walls had dwindled.

Out there, somewhere, like satellites in space, were other worlds, sealed like their own. Their daughter, now in New Zealand, still safe, but far, far away. And their son, who had not visited for years; who barely even phoned. The old story, worn with retelling.

IV

'Do you really think we should?' he asked. He often looked to her for approval of a plan.

She paused, closed her eyes for a moment to think, then nodded again. 'Yes.'

'In other times, we'd have offered it to a – a museum, or…'

'Those times have…'

'Gone,' they said together.

They were silent for a little while. They did not often discuss the Crisis, as people now called it: the slow unravelling of systems – agricultural, economic, political, social, cultural – brought on by human greed and carelessness. A gradual collapse of continuity and certainty. It was too much to confront.

He looked out through the window, where the sun was edging below the horizon. Such beauty. Like a strand of hope.

She gazed at the tabletop, so solid and dependable, despite all the demands and burdens they had placed on it over so many years. Bearing the marks of long use. Like him, she thought, affectionately.

They were still alive, still breathing, still sitting at their old kitchen table. As if nothing had changed.

V

She imagined the flavour, dry at first, then muskily sweet, with a sharp, oily undercurrent. Her mouth began to water slightly.

'Shall we – ?' Again, they spoke the same words at almost the same moment. So long together.

She reached for the nutcrackers.

'Wait,' he said. He smiled, and she admired the wrinkles amid the furze of his white beard.

'What?'

'Let's try to keep it whole.'

She smiled, and he admired the glint in her watery eyes.

She placed the walnut between the jaws of the nutcrackers, carefully centring it, and began to squeeze, gently but firmly.

'Wait,' he said again. He disappeared into the passage. She heard the click of the old light switch in his tool cupboard.

VI

About five years ago, perhaps longer, she had noticed a small, down-page story in the paper. Walnut growers in Iran were expressing concern over a new blight devastating their crops. Livelihoods were threatened. Anger was mounting over government inaction.

She had barely registered it. There was always a new threat: a beetle, a fungus, a virus. There were always lazy or corrupt public officials, failing to act. But she learned that the Persian walnut was also the English walnut. The same species as their tree.

Over time, the story grew larger and wider. Walnut trees were dying out, not just in Iran but in the larger producing nations, where other species grew: China, the United States, Canada.

They went out to examine their tree. They felt the green, glossy leaves between their fingers, looked for black dots, prised away little chunks of bark. Nothing.

The headlines now spoke of 'Walnut wipeout'.

VII

She dreamed of a planet, spinning lazily through space. On its surface, and below its skin, life burgeoned and swelled, but it was constrained by a hard outer shell. The planet lumbered on blindly through its orbit, quivering with the internal pressure. She watched it slowly dwindling into the infinite distance.

He dreamed he was running through a forest, thick and dark with dying trees. The trees sighed and groaned as the life drained from them. Their leaves writhed, blackened and curled like grasping fingers. As he forced his way through the mesh of doomed branches he became aware of smoke, billowing and thickening between the trunks. Then came sparks, then orange tongues of flame. He turned to escape but found himself surrounded. He woke, gasping in the night.

VIII

He returned to the kitchen holding a large iron vice, grimed with rust. She sighed in mock exasperation. 'Appliance of science,' he grinned.

He set the vice on the table. It would not lie flat. It was designed to be clamped to a workbench. She had seen it attached to the kitchen table before. She remembered chiding him as she wiped away grubby marks.

He hummed quietly as he tightened the clamps, then tenderly placed the walnut between the iron jaws, aligning it to apply pressure along the seam.

He wound the lever on the vice slowly, until suddenly the nutshell split. It came apart in shards, not the two neat halves he had hoped for. But the nut inside was still whole. The broken shell clung to the gnarled interior. He reached for it.

'Let me,' she said, darting out her hand, brushing away his fat, clumsy fingers.

IX

Their tree seemed in rude health, despite all the dire prophecies. They began to wonder if they were custodians of a phenomenon. Might their tree, with its apparent resistance to the blight, offer a lifeline for the survival of the species? It seemed unlikely, but they contacted the botanical gardens.

Inspectors arrived within two days. They were polite and enthusiastic, but also business-like. They put on white overalls, blue overshoes and blue gloves. They even wore surgical masks. They carried ladders, specialist tools and plastic sample boxes.

For two hours, the botanists scrutinised the tree. They climbed its upper boughs, plucked its leaves, tweaked off a few of its ripening nuts, sheared its bark, drilled into its trunk, took samples from the surrounding soil, photographed it at close range and at full height. Then, with tight smiles, they left.

X

She teased out the pieces of shell, one at a time, carefully prising them from the crinkled brown flesh, working out the fragments of dark, bitter husk. Triumphantly, she pulled the last piece free, leaving the nut exposed and whole, tightly contoured like the two halves of a small brain. A man's brain, she thought, and tittered.

'What?' he said, surprised and curious.

'Nothing,' she said, playful and reassuring.

Smiling, she placed it on her palm and held it out to him. 'Look.

They stared at it together, admiring its perfection.

XI

One of the botanists called a few days later. He answered the phone.

'I'm sorry,' said a gentle female voice. 'Not what we'd hoped. This year's crop is healthy – you can eat the nuts without any risk. But, well, it's unlikely you'll get another.'

'Oh,' he said, 'so it's – ?'

'Yes, it's in the early stages of the disease. But it advances quite rapidly. I'm sorry.' She sounded it.

XII

'I feel we should… record it,' he said suddenly.

'Record?' she said, more surprised than scornful. 'How can you record a taste?'

'No, I mean… in writing.'

'Oh. Oh yes, of course. That's a good idea, love.' She touched his hand, apologetic; encouraging.

He went and fetched a pen and an old notebook. He tested the pen, found it working, and smoothed the pages open. Then he said, 'Ready?'

She nodded. He gently prised the two halves of the walnut apart. Then he offered one half to her. 'Eat,' he said.

It was a ceremony, a roleplay, a surrogacy. The nut must represent all walnuts, and they all human mouths.

They ate it. The last walnut.

She brought a crumpled tissue to her thin, pale cheek. He took the pen and began to write.

Trinity Park

by Sherry Cassells

Longlisted, Edinburgh Short Story Award 2025

Seven Bells

They are studying homelessness at the high school, that's what the kid said, as if it's a thing on a petri dish.

He spoke through the fence from where he stood on the sidewalk. He wasn't dressed for the weather, he was shivering, first week of November you need more than a school blazer.

In white words he asked if I'd help him with his project.

Mine was the only fire going, light was just sparking up between the buildings on one side and the trees on the other. I could have said anything back to him, or nothing at all, I could have told him to get lost and I might have, but just then a grapefruit flew between us like a breakneck sun.

It came from Saint Rose, *I'd rather get scurvy,* she yelled.

The kid said some idiot in his class probably gave her the fruit as a bribe, he said everybody wanted to interview Saint Rose.

I told the kid to tell his friend Saint Rose preferred her fruit fermented.

Seven bells peeled, he looked in their direction, he rather *absorbed* them, and when they quieted he said it again,

127

earnestly through the fence as if I hadn't heard the first time, *we are exploring homelessness.*

I shrugged and said, *me too.*

Project's due tomorrow.

Don't they teach you anything? – my words also white – *tomorrow never comes.*

He asked if I would keep a diary of my day, and again I could have said anything, nothing, a pomegranate flew by, I reached for the bag he offered and placed it on the ground in front of me.

Thank you. I'll be back same time tomorrow.

Something else went by, similar to a lime but probably an avocado, it hit my retreating student in the shoulder and fell to the ground a pear.

We call it a church but it is a Gothic cathedral with 12 change ringing bells. Its spire was once the tallest structure in Canada and it does not lose its grandness in spite of the neighbouring stacked and gleaming giants, its white brick and sandstone walls absorb the light, maybe some sins, it glows.

We used to pile into its paupers' cemetery at night, we'll end up there anyway so not *trespassing* like they said, more like *practicing,* but they have made it inhospitable. Armrests have been installed on the benches denoting individual seats, they prevent us from laying down but give the impression of portioned-out generosity.

Little bright bulbs like falling stars but grapes, a galaxy of them land at my feet, the idiot who wanted the interview with Saint Rose pelts by, I say *thanks for the grapes* to her shape. They are cold and hard and sweet.

Things are starting to change here, it's like the depiction of dawn in a musical, all the tents open at once and people stretch and yawn from them, there's an incohesiveness, a chaos that looks like it could snap into something choreographed, Gloria at the edge of the forest fencing with her umbrella, one-handed Marcus in a warrior two variation, a few others pushing and pulling, something of a rhythm comes, fires are lit, and here we are, in the combined glow of morning.

Somebody shouts out their madness, somebody else says, *shut up, Harry.*

Such is life in Trinity Park, where tomorrow comes every single day to those of us who thought it never would.

Nine Bells

Here beneath the clouds I am Trinity's gatekeeper. Criteria for admission are somewhat arbitrary, but for denial they are precise.

At nine bells dawn is over and we are looking for something else, the alcohol and drug seekers lurch away, other groups fray, the rest of us go it alone, our searches individual. Mine is to find my poetic self, the one whose heart beats with ferocious passion, the one who would have been a playwright, for make no mistake, we are all artists, we homeless in Trinity Park.

Where do you think your gatekeepers rest?

Twelve Bells

I would have been a playwright.

Something like: A single beam of light on a size seven sweater hangs on the back of a chair in a hollow room. The owner of the sweater is missing. Her mother, by the window's early light, picks the sweater up, sits in the chair, threads a needle and stitches along the sweater's edges. The turquoise thread melts into the turquoise wool, she remembers knitting it, purposefully large, her strategy backfired and the sweater, forgotten until this year, is now a poor fit, her daughter's delicate wrist bones rise like stones from the final row of knit-one-pearl-two stitches. When she looks out the window she places the top button into her mouth and sucks its clacking shape, the sweater hangs from her lips and down her throat, it widens at her stomach and narrows into her lap, pawing. She tries to remember if her daughter mentioned a double sleepover, she looks down the road watching for the girl to come to her like thread through a needle.

We time. We count in secret. Will the body before ours be the final to cascade into the cathedral ground? When will they say *when*. We count cigarettes and coins, clouds, birds, we count empty bottles, years, and we count the bells, we believe we are for whom they toll, we hope there is room for one more, we are neither -full nor -less, hope's proportions are various as the clouds, the starlings that give, at this time of year, shape to the sky.

One Bell

There is a woman who says, *I am so far away from home,*
into the space between her and everyone who passes, the
words travel through the fence, she says it in the same
way others ask for spare change. I think people would
rather hand over what's in their pockets than what is in,
or not in, their hearts. She makes the office girls with their
shoes and handbags think of home, their ageing mothers
who iron in the next room, the window through which
sheep sway over knitted green fields, their father's
miniature shape seems to stride along the windowsill.

Trinity Park is not entirely fenced in, we have 180 degrees
of free forest that tumbles into a ravine after which the
birch rise again and thin, for a few flat miles only grass
rolls, and then railroad tracks – show me a homeless
heart that is not stirred by the whistle of a train – and
then Lake Ontario. We know of its wildness but see no
evidence, from here it looks contained under glass,
impossibly gigantic ships appear, one wonders how they
stay afloat, the office girls who walk along the sidewalk
on the other side of the fence feel the same about the old
men who gaze at these ships as if lending them
buoyancy, they wonder how the men stay alive.

Nocturnal Matik yells in her sleep, her teepee in full sun
now, she pleads for a canoe. Every night she tells the
same tale of when she was forced into a boat that took her
from her home on the reserve to assumed safety, her
mother yelled from the shore for her to sit backwards and
memorize the way, this was Lake of the Woods,
brimming with islands, Matik says even now she could

get home if only she had a canoe, that the islands are fixed behind her eyes, when she walks, she paddles.

There is a knot of women who gather at one bell upon a picnic bench that has been burned in the centre, they are the trolls at our gates, my helpers – they keep the gawkers away while I consider the candidates – their stringy hair and fattened bodies roll and smash together, clothing like seaweed, they are a coven of toothless wretches, they shout and laugh at those who work across the street, the ambitious young, who they say will one day take their place.

One bell reminds us of our loneliness.

I warm soup in an iron pot that hangs over my fire, they come to it with tin cups like a Dickens' story, like we are acting in a renaissance play, many of us forget the audition, we don't know quite how we landed the part.

Homelessness is not a condition nor a profession but an art.

Four Bells

I spy my student, he is younger than he seemed this morning. I wonder how he sees me, my beard blackly pointing toward the ships, my own *I am so far away from home* in its furls. Is it possible he sees me as the playwright I would have been, my poetic stanzas all lined up, sometimes I want the words to be less perfect, less proper, my education betrays my heart, I want to say things as they are and leave the superfluous, I want to say *fuck off* and I end up saying *fuck thee off.*

I hunch to my work, the wind to and fro in my straining mouth.

Four bells is when the door to sanity starts to close, the other door is also closed, we are in a variation of purgatory, not unlike the warm space between the doors to the barroom, the one behind us closed against the winterous outdoors, the other closed, we wait.

The skies are porous, perilous – *when will the darkness?*

Eight Bells

At eight bells Harry's madness torques, Saint Rose spreads curses, Marcus feels for his pulse with his missing hand, our trolls haggle, the skeleton of Gloria's umbrella spiders away, Matik madly paddles, the ragged forest barely distinguishable from the sky, sirens on the other side, trains roar.

I retreat into my tent like a child into his bedroom when his parents start tearing discontent into objects they lob, one skids down the hallway and comes to unrest in the strip of light beneath the door, it finds its way under the beds of the young, and the discontent continues.

My student will return tomorrow morning at seven bells and I will hand my pages over to him, my careful words designed to add weight to his bones and allow no monsters beneath.

Seven Bells

My tent is plunged into light, its sensitive skin glows from the bottom up, there are no rips but scars, soon the bells will soften into snow and during those harsh and beautiful months their peels do not reach us.

Do they toll for thee?

Spring will once more come like a blessing and our trolls will frolic, Saint Rose will scurry through the city and return rich, Matik will cry out, we remember our far away homes, our mothers in the next room, our fathers in the fields, the floating sheep, the ships will continue, the shivering city, the trains through our shoulders.

I pack my pages into the bag like an inheritance, further advice waits in my mouth.

He hears what I say in the same way he listened to the seven bells yesterday, he *ingests* my words, I tell him to notice *all* of life and its peoples – the forests! the cities! the churches! the graveyards! the cries! the whispers! the skies! the seas!

I tell him to know the way home all his blessed grapefruit days.

I angle the bag through the fence, he thanks me and walks away, he turns and looks at me with electricity and I know he understands that life is no less a miracle when seen from the inside of a pale and worn tent.

"I had observed that the men who were most in life, who were molding life, who were life itself, ate little, slept little, owned little or nothing. They had no illusions about duty... or the preservation of the State. They were interested in truth and in truth alone."

Henry Miller, The Rosy Crucifixion: Sexus, Plexus, Nexus (1949)

Gunnerson's Wardrobe

by Peter Court

Longlisted, Edinburgh Short Story Award 2025

Young Gunnerson has lost his beloved fishtail chisel. It was just there at his elbow, in reach, as he shaped the wooden frame, smoothing the edges, perfecting the snug fit of the precious dark timber pieces. Mr. Hampton will be furious. The workshop, small with grey salt windows peering out onto a street of turtle cobbles. A golden light makes the room of wood dust and saw oil seem magical. Young Gunnerson has developed something of a reputation for misplacing valuable tools. But also, to be entirely fair to the wiry lad, Mr. Hampton is pretty much always furious. His boss is a compacted granite nugget of tooth breaking hardness. More than anything, Young Gunnerson wants Mr. Hampton to respect him. Instead, the old man has a cliff faced scowl that he reserves just for his skeletal young apprentice. With a clutching in his gut, Young Gunnerson looks exactly where the fishtail chisel should be. Right there, inside the big scent filled body of the furniture piece. What is now its floor but, when Young Gunnerson has finished his work, will become the back of the tall, sturdy, and very bespoke wardrobe. But the valuable tool has gone. Vanished.

And here is where we can focus in and explore Young Gunnerson's problem. Fifteen years ago, his family packed dry wooden crates and moved to this soft land with its convoluted language and the feeling of people constantly untucked and flapping in the chill. Young Gunnerson is a passionate believer in the Christ he found in his mother's stories, told long ago, far away. What had grabbed little Gunnerson, before he grew into Young Gunnerson, was the strange man who walked through a crowd of screaming, pounding faces. His mother would make these walks come alive.

'Heal my mother Yah Shua, Give me sight again, Bring wealth to my pockets' the people would shout, pressing in on the little bearded rabbi, the crowd pressing in and heaving like a beast. But he is soft. Quiet. Just walking.

Little Gunnerson would sit, enraptured.

'And then in all the turmoil,' his mother would whisper, 'the great teacher would stop and tilt his head to one side and say, "Hm, someone just touched me," and all of the people would say "No joke Rabbi. Who DIDN'T touch you!" But he ignored them. That is the way he always walked gently in the turmoil.'

Little Gunnerson would be leaning forward now, even though he knew exactly where the story was going. Because a classic tale, well told, always brings you forward.

'The mighty little fellow turned slowly and there, behind him, was a woman, kneeling in his shadow. No one in the crowd even saw her. But him, he felt her, and he knew what she needed.'

That was the little rabbi who walked thousands of miles, thousands of years, to sit at their table in poverty-stricken Gelsenkirchen, a decade before the beginning of the first great and terrible war. Little Gunnerson met the man of peace just before his entire homeland, the whole of Europe, fell into a quagmire of hate and death. His mother, his father, his two sisters, were able to flee from the terrible machines of war. But not for long. Little Gunnerson would grow to play a massive role in the ultimate battle. But first he must lose this beloved fishtail chisel.

Mr. Hampton looks like a heart attack. Ruddy cheeks and the fine lines on his nose that have collected over beer glasses. Many, many, beer glasses. He hasn't always been so marked and short tempered. His is a world of business and making. Running the little furniture store on Blackthorn Lane is a skill, a craft he learned at the calloused hands of his imposing father. He is not as good as his father was. Mr. Hampton, the stumbling junior, now feels that those same calloused hands of his father are holding him down. As the business lurches from moments of great success to the long lean stretches between commissions, he has become an unsettled and constantly fearful man. Fortunately, Mr.Hampton is not alone in this business. He was wise enough to see the magical skill in the hands of the young lad called Gunnerson who now amazes the clients with the beauty and craftsmanship of his slender young hands. All of which just makes Mr. Hampton even more threatened. More fearful. More angry.

'ow can ye lose another bloody tool. Chroist!' the angry boss throws the words into the belly of the workshop. Young Gunnerson flinches.

'It vas just there Mr. Hampton. Und please don't with the name of my Lord.'

'What! You lose my expensive tools and you think I care about your stupid dead Jew?'

Young Gunnerson draws a deep breath and waits for his hands to stop shaking so he can tell Mr. Hampton why he is so wrong about the wonderful Rabbi. This would be a foolish thing to do right now. But that has never stopped Young Gunnerson. Possibly Young Gunnerson was too passionate. You've met them right? 'Have you heard my favourite song? You *have* to read this book! How can you *not* love; [insert their *team/colour/Royal family] here*?' Or the most troubling of all; 'You have to love my God, let me tell you why.' Yes, Young Gunnerson arrived in England with a garlic sausage accent, neatly manicured skin and the deep belief that everyone should believe precisely as he believes. This simply makes Mr. Hampton scowl and throw more gravel at the boy. Hampton is a jealous man. But more so, he is angry, made so by the fear of his business shrinking, fear of his skin greying, fear of the grumble from across the channel of the engines of war. History will show that Mr. Hampton is right to fear. Not for his business. In a decade or so, the next time a new generation of war machines grind across the channel, his little furniture workshop will play an important role churning out beautifully crafted air frames for the DeHavilland aircraft company. Nor should he be concerned about his greying skin because Mr. Hampton's life is ordered by a power well beyond his acid tongue and graceless chin. In fact, this little pine and musk workshop will be under his scowling eye for a very long time. However, those war machines across the channel today, one day soon they will snatch his magical young apprentice and thrust him, a skinny, terrified German-born carpentry apprentice, into a British uniform, to be slaughtered in a French trench. But that is a fear for the future. Young Gunnerson doesn't know he is ready to face that death, all he knows is he wants to tell people of this Rabbi he found in a dank Teutonic kitchen. Whether they want to hear him or not.

And so we come to Elizabeth Hampton. She began her life as Elizabeth Saint James. She is a small girl on the outside, but within her is a universe. The heart within her demands more than just beating and blood. She thrives on greater things. She lost many of her early years wandering the pages of novels of the time. The stunning new worlds of Mr. Verne, the rustle and crimple of the Bronte's. Her heart soared to wuthering heights and flew to *A Princess of Mars*. To her glaring mother she was a bookworm, a child wasting away on a sunlit bench in the garden. But from these pages she drew a nectar that shaped her own future. She loved things new, things never seen before. Things created. So the first time she walked past Hampton's of Blackthorn Lane and saw, through the window, the beautifully turned legs of young Mister Hampton's bedside table, she was smitten. Elizabeth became Mrs. Hampton and soon was embroiled in the day-to-day business of trying to make a little furniture shop into a family business. For him it is all he ever knew. For her it was the future for her son. As she watches the apprentice, she often has a far-away face, a sigh. Sometimes a tear. She loves the way the boy talks to his work. He doesn't make furniture, he embraces it. Brings it forth. Conjures it. Like magic. And he makes the boss's wife cry. The clumsy, quiet young German boy has become a solid joy in her life. A boy in her home. The one thing she needs from her husband that he has been unable to provide. This, more than anything, makes Mr. Hampton small, fearful and angry.

In the aftermath of the missing fishtail chisel, she brings Young Gunnerson tea and speaks with soft maternal assurance.

'Don't you pay no heed to Mr 'Ampton, 'e's just a grumpy old bugger.' She tells him as they sit and sip. He is propped against the ancient bench with the archaeology of scratches and stains. She sits primly at the little desk in the corner where the paperwork collects. The thin German boy sighs.

'Vy can't he just see zat zere is a whole vorld, of joy und vonder, if only he vill take a moment to see it.'

'Well, see, I don't think he can see much past 'is own nose, you know?' and they both chuckle. 'So I reckon,' she sips as she considers. 'I reckon 'e don't want to see, see? I think our Mr 'Ampton is 'appy bein' the grumpy old bugger. An' if he weren't, I don't know if 'e'd know 'imslef.'

Young Gunnerson looks at the little woman with the glowing face.

'Vat about you? Do you vant more zan this vorld?'

'Ah, well, young lad, don't you worry 'bout me. I've got me books, I've got me 'ome. I reckon I'm pretty plum.'

With a spare sanding block now, Young Gunnerson is back at work. His frustration drives him to confide in the ornate heart of the wardrobe.

'Jah, you know, I am a failure.' He drives his arms, pouring energy and frustration into the wood. 'I vant so much to speak truth but all I do is make things Vorse. Why can I not make him belief like I belief?'

Young Gunnerson is so engrossed in his magical making that he will never see the effect of his work. Too tangled in what he sees as his uselessness, too frustrated that his boiling wonder completely fails to convince even Mr. Hampton of the power of the faith he holds. What the boy believes is that his words fall like dead leaves, spent, unheeded, good only for mulch and compost. But his hands, they speak too. He doesn't hear. Doesn't know. That this wardrobe, like all of the furniture he creates, this wardrobe is something special. This wardrobe has a voice, has a place in history. It soon will tell a story that will change millions of lives. If only Young Gunnerson realised, he might not be so anxious about his words, his value, or about the precious fishtail chisel that now lies on the snows of the mythical land of Narnia.

The Bread Servers' Tale

by J N Ian Dickson

Longlisted, Edinburgh Short Story Award 2025

Solomon knows a thing or two. Horses do. The route for each day except Sunday is embedded in his hooves. No work on a Sunday. Double manna on a Saturday. A biblical pattern in play for generations, a well-worn sequence in these parts. Six days labour, one day rest; if you can get labour that is.

William James fits the pattern. He works for the big bakery, and grateful for it. It is a steady job but physically strenuous on the road in all weathers. He hopes that his children, if he has any, won't have to work as physically hard as their father. William, at the age of twenty, is a custodian of a societal belief in progress. He is better off than his father. So, his son or sons will be better off than him. And their sons, in turn, ad infinitum. But he is wise enough not to view it as inevitable, especially in 1940, as a bloody war rages across France.

William and Solomon serve bread. It is a reserved profession, a vital service industry in the war effort. They move through the countryside by road, lane and track, across fields, to bring fresh bread to families whose husbands and sons are away at war, and to the elderly, now too frail to fight or bake. For some country folk it is a step too far. To buy bakery bread from a server is, for a rural traditionalist, a betrayal. 'Not as good as griddle bread', they insist, when William calls to find new people to serve.

Solomon hears William's steps on the tiles of the bakery depot and turns his head in welcome before a bouncy nod.

'Morning Solomon!' William says, reaching a hand out to stroke his mane.

'Frost on the ground, old boy. Slippery roads. A cold one to go north! But north we must go!'

William has a deep friendship with this horse. They are mates and confidantes. Human and equine, they are partners. Solomon tolerates William's little ways and moods. William, on his part, looks after Solomon as he would a king. But the harsh roads and weathering in all seasons is hard on them both. The journey back to the depot each night is taking longer and longer. To William it makes no sense to go so far on Tuesdays and Thursdays, so north to the very coast and back so south again. But who is he to say. He does his job; the horse does his.

'Now, Solomon, let's get the bread loaded and you hitched up.'

William throws his bag containing a few slices of buttered loaf, a chunk of cheese and a flask of tea onto the seat of the bakery cart.

'I wonder how Ginny Wallace is after the news of her son's death. Picked off by sniper fire, they said. Nowhere is safe in war, Solomon. She must be devastated, with the death of her only brother just last month.'

Solomon replies with a swing of his head and a nuzzle into William's arm. 'Humans', he must wonder, 'are strange creatures. Fighting and killing each other all the time. Making up stories to frighten people. They laugh weirdly, too.'

Most country folk treat the horse as an old ancestor, with kindness, water and food. For they too are ageing. A bit stiff, looking down more often these days to check their footing. To fall and break a leg on the farm would be a serious business, as Solomon knows only too well.

'They try to fix you, but they shoot me,' Solomon might say, if asked.

The hand-painted maroon livery on the bakery cart is inscribed, in blue lettering, 'McMillan Bakers – Fresh Bread on your Doorstep.' William is a master packer, using every square inch. Struggled with school arithmetic but he has a natural eye for volume. Each loaf he squeezes so gently, imperceptibly testing it, subconsciously filtering for freshness. He travels highroads and byways with pride, entering yards and houses, big and small, kept and unkept. For young William, it is about people not bread. The bread server and his horse deliver humanity.

The first stop is an open yard, wide enough to turn the cart with ease. The backdoor of the farmhouse lies open. William can't recall ever seeing it shut.

'Anybody home!' William hollers as he steps down from the cart. Underfoot is wet, the cobbles glisten.

'There's always somebody home. You know that...
William James!' The voice from within responds, as if on
cue.

William leaves Solomon to rest in the yard and steps into
the large kitchen, and then through it to a sitting room
where an old man is seated next to the hearth.

'I've brought you two batch loaves as usual and thrown
in an apple pie just made yesterday by my aunt. No extra
cost.'

'You're a good fella, William James.'

'How are things?' William replies to Jim Buchanan.

William uses this question (or a version of it) on a daily
basis with his *clients*. A raw and unfortunate business
term, favoured by the Bakery management, which he
finds wholly inappropriate for his practice of delivering
humanity.

'The question, ah – I learnt it from Jesus,' he told a young
lad once. The boy had been assigned to help William,
after a leg injury inflicted by Solomon. The horse in those
early days of their partnership kicked William, who had
inadvertently approached from behind. 'A case of
mistaken identity', William liked to think.

'From Jesus?' The young lad queried.

'Yes, these two travellers were walking on a road. It was
hot. They were upset. A stranger joins them and sees
them a bit confused. To get them talking, Jesus asks this
question. When they say to him, "Don't you know what
things are happening here?" he says to them, "What

things?" And they tell him how things are for them. He listens to their story.'

William continued his reflections on the importance of everyone's story and got quite emotional thinking of people who have no one to listen to them. He feared they might think they are nobodies.

The young lad asked no more.

Jim Buchanan is in full flight of speech, pushing a giant log into the fire with his right leather boot, as every three inches or so burns off. He is no longer fit to cut wood. William is treated to an array of local news, bulletins on Jim's health, the death notices in the newspaper, comment on the requisition of land for the war effort, and an update on the prices of animal feed. From the hearth, Jim is in the loop. To top it all, he announces that his son, who left the farm for a city job, is coming home any day now.

'Maybe Charlie will take the farm, William!' Jim shows no emotion, but inside he is like a child at Christmas.

William leaves Jim having brewed a pot of tea and cut a slice of apple pie, placing it within easy reach by the fire. Prior to this, Jim briefly paused his stories, for a repeated rite of passage, initiated on William's first call at the house as a mere sixteen year old.

'My hands are too shaky, young lad.' William recalls the words as if it were yesterday.

He remembers being sent into the dank bathroom and returning with an open razor, soap and brush to begin shaving Jim Buchanan.

Reuniting with Solomon in the yard, William steps up, takes the reins and moves off.

'See you soon, Jim'. He shouts through the open door.

No reply. Williams imagines his mouth is already full of apple pie.

Next call is Ginny Wallace. On his first visit to Ginny, William was treated to a bowl of homemade cereal, kept in a brown paper bag in the pantry. As she prepared it, he noticed a hole in one corner spilling out a little mound of cereal that Ginny seemed not to notice. The hole spooked William. It was almost certainly crafted by hungry mice. He remembers enjoying mouthfuls of cereal in a rather pungent buttermilk, but only after he buried the hole in the back of his mind. It was her kind act; it said, 'you are one of us.'

Ginny's yard is smaller, but Solomon has the measure of it. The story is that when her brother and son went to the second war and she was left alone things became unmanageable. The first war had 'stolen Thomas', as she put it, her husband of twenty years. He came home right enough, but within a year he was in a mental institution miles away. Never recovered. She ran the farm with her brother and son. Then, they too were called up.

William is anxious about how things are. He must be careful with his words. For news of young Tom's death is fresh, barely a month on from the shock of Jack's death.

Ginny's door is shut. An old dog lies curled up in a corner near the byre. It could be dead or alive, it's hard to tell. William strokes Solomon's mane, in response he whinnies and angles his head as if to say, 'I know. But you must go in.'

William gathers her bread order from the back of the cart. No additions until he sees how the land lies.

'Ginny, are you there?' He calls out, raising the latch on the back door. It opens into a short passage William knows well. He steps in.

'It's William, with your bread!' He continues, moving towards the living room. That door is open but no one is there.

Now at the foot of the stairs, he calls again.

No sound.

He returns to the yard.

'Perhaps she is in the byre or the old outhouse at the edge of the back field,' he wonders, striding out.

'Ginny, are you ...'

William stops mid-sentence when he catches sight of Ginny, appearing round the corner of the byre. He is closing on her. She looks gaunt, her unwashed hair pinned back with kirby grips. Her eyes stare out. Her arms hang, devoid of natural strength. Shoulders stooped. In her hands is a shotgun – double-barrelled, recently fired, pointed down, expended.

'The bastard ...,' she calls out.

'... Who? What's happened, Ginny?' William speaks quickly.

As he reaches out to take the weight of the gun for her, she snatches it away from him.

'That bastard Nazi, that's who!' Ginny, the god-fearing woman, turns back into the byre. William follows.

'There he is,' she scowls, using the weapon to point out a man's body lying in a pool of blood on the ground, 'the bastard Nazi that killed my Tom!'

Ginny drops the shotgun. She stands rigid.

This man isn't a Nazi, William is sure of that.

The body makes no movement. He is dead. The shotgun showed no mercy.

William shakes as he moves closer to the man.

'Who is he then? A prowler? A burglar?' William's mind is flashing with options. He read somewhere that since the war began burglary is on the increase, men being away and all that. Easy pickings.

'You can't just shoot people, Ginny.' His voice to his own ears is scratchy, high-pitched and his words sound ridiculous.

'Tom. Jack. Thomas.' Ginny says each name with a strong intonation into the empty echoey space.

The body is face down. William feels a familiarity, but there is no time left to wonder why. Touching the left shoulder, he automatically squeezes it. This bread is stale. A glimpse at the face, even in part profile, makes William reel back and rise to his full stature.

'This is no Nazi, Ginny,' he says turning to her. 'It's Charlie ...,' William's voice cracks.

'... Jim Buchanan's son.'

No words reach Ginny now. No tears.

Charlie heard about Tom and, on his way home, he called to pay his respects.

'I'm sorry for your loss' were his last words.

Orchard and Fog

by Priyanka Kumra

Longlisted, Edinburgh Short Story Award 2025

September 1974. Sometimes I see it like a polaroid developing in slow motion. The Victorian house on Pine Ridge Road looms above the Sacramento Valley, where morning tule creeps in like a half-forgotten promise. The house itself – weathered redwood bones and wide bay windows – leans into the wind as though bracing for something no one can name.

Inside that house, in a kitchen with hexagonal tiles, stands my mother: Amma. I remember the way the edge of her sari brushes the floor, though at nine years old I never thought to call it remarkable. She has turmeric stains on her hands, a grey cardigan twisted between her fingers. Later I'd realize how thoroughly she'd absorbed that small, Western gesture of worry.

We left Chennai when I was nine. That's a fact. Another fact: memory is trickier than geography. When I recall our old family compound in India, it's as changeable as the tule – teeming with aunts, uncles, and cousins one moment, empty hallways echoing with Radio Ceylon the next.

Appa, my father, insisted we take in a lodger. 'There is no other way to make some extra money,' he said, but something else lingered in his voice. Maybe a need to prove we belonged here in this slant of unfamiliar sunlight, in a land where everything felt like it had been tilted five degrees off-center. He said all this at our kitchen table, fingers drumming against walnut laminate, eyes glued to that same tabletop rather than meeting Amma's gaze. Amma stood at the sink, outlined by the window that framed row upon row of almond orchards stretching into mist.

Our front steps – fifteen of them – led up to the house like a question that must be answered every day. Each morning I'd climb them carefully, counting each one with the solemnity of a ritual. I didn't know then that each of us was testing our own form of gravity, each trying not to slip.

Frankie arrived on a Wednesday. When I think back, I recall the way autumn light bent around her tall figure, flared jeans swishing with each step, a guitar case plastered with stickers of places I couldn't pinpoint on a map: Austin, Nashville, Portland, Seattle. Amma had prepared the space like someone expecting a sacred visitor – incense stuck into halved potatoes lining the entry, brass vessels polished to a mirrored gleam, sandalwood competing with the scent of crushed bay leaves outside. Even at nine, I could sense the hush.

For weeks, I watched Frankie move about our house as if testing its edges – leaning in doorframes, propping her boots on the coffee table, throwing back her head to laugh at something my parents wouldn't quite understand. Her guitar case claimed the attic room, silent yet alive with possibility, the missing chords of an America we couldn't fully touch.

Certain images still cling to my mind: Amma at the stove, the pressure cooker exhaling clouds of steam. Appa crouched behind his newspaper fortress each morning, meticulously spreading grape jelly – never jam – on toast. Frankie's cigarette smoke drifting through the attic floorboards, a scent that felt both forbidden and oddly comforting.

Outside, the almond orchards cycled through their own transformations. In September, mechanical shakers rattled nuts from the branches in a sound like falling hail. By October, the trees turned skeletal against a sky that shifted from pewter to pale silver. The first frost arrived in November, layering everything in a quiet hush. Time was different here. In Chennai, holy bells and visiting relatives gave structure to each day. In this Californian valley, we measured life by weather patterns and Frankie's late shifts at The Frontier Bar.

Autumn evenings at our house always shimmer in my memory. Amma cooking 'ordinary dishes,' except they were rich with hidden meaning – subtle spice combinations cooking down into conversation starters. Frankie stood at the kitchen table, leaning over the steel masala dabba in a way that made everything else look smaller. She'd ask, 'What makes each spice special?' Her voice was gravelly, as though it had spent too many nights singing in smoky bars. Amma answered in her measured English, each word carefully delivered like a pinch of cumin measured out in a spoon.

Patterns formed with enviable regularity. I'd come home from school and see Frankie's hand resting on Amma's shoulder for a heartbeat longer than instruction required.

Sometimes their laughter would stop cold when I walked in, as if I'd interrupted a conversation they couldn't share with me. The surest sign of all: one of Amma's ruby earrings surfacing in Frankie's room, a stray glint under the pillow. I knew whose it was. I just didn't know what to do with that knowledge.

Appa seemed too preoccupied – or too determined to remain uninvolved – to notice. He left for the Sacramento insurance office early, returned late, complaining of endless forms, stubborn clients, and the thick tule that swallowed entire roads. If he and Frankie spoke, it was only about rent, or the water heater that needed fiddling, or the way the front steps sometimes groaned under the morning dew.

The accident came on a Monday in November. I still dream about it sometimes. Amma was driving our Dodge Dart, Frankie in the passenger seat, and I sat in the back, fiddling with the radio knob. The tule that morning was thick as milk. One moment the road was empty. The next – a truck filled with orchard workers burst into view, all chrome and sound. Metal found metal in a scream that reverberated through my bones.

A moment before impact, I'd glimpsed Frankie's hand on Amma's thigh. Then a sharp intake of breath. Then chaos.

Hospitals can smell like raw fear. Mine did, with disinfectant stinging my nostrils. My chin needed seven stitches – I've traced them with my fingers repeatedly since then, like reading braille. Appa arrived looking dazed in his work clothes, tie askew. He moved past me and toward Amma with mechanical efficiency, signing forms, nodding without hearing. I don't remember him

154

saying my name. I don't remember anyone mentioning Frankie. Just hushed voices and the rustling of white jackets.

By dawn the next day, Frankie was gone. She left three things: her guitar case, with a folded note tucked inside – 'Little Bird – keep this safe for me. Some songs need time to find their ending,' – the faint odor of Marlboro smoke in the attic, and a silence between Amma and Appa so heavy it felt like the air was pressing on my ears.

The house on Pine Ridge Road felt bigger without Frankie, but emptier, too. The almond trees, stripped bare for winter, looked like black skeletons etched against the sky. We still set the table each night, still performed the rituals of mealtime. But I felt it: a slow leak of warmth that no one acknowledged.

That first morning after Frankie disappeared, I walked alone to the bus stop. Tule swallowed the valley. I glanced back, half-convinced the house might vanish in the white wash behind me. It looked fragile from that angle, like a secret that could be erased with a single breath.

This is what I told myself: It's just another morning.

This is what I knew: Nothing would ever be just anything again.

Winter descended, bringing new rules of absence. Amma took off her ruby earrings and never spoke of them. The guitar case in the attic gathered dust, as if it were an artifact in a museum no one dared open. Silence became a living thing, changing shape with every room it entered. In the kitchen, Amma polished the same steel pot far longer than necessary, eyes distant. In the living room, Appa hid behind his newspaper, flipping pages so methodically it sounded like a clock ticking. I learned to be quiet in a way that felt grown-up.

In December, I found Appa at the dining table with his head in his hands, the overhead light casting sharp shadows on his face. 'It's just more forms,' he muttered, voice cracking in the middle of the sentence. A part of me realized this was the first time I'd seen him look lost. When he noticed me, he straightened the stack of papers, forced a smile I didn't believe, and returned to the refuge of his pen. That was my glimpse into the small, frightened chamber of his heart.

The trees outside our window, once so lush, now stood in their winter dormancy: tall silhouettes on frosted ground, branches shaped like haiku, spare and haunting. Without the weekly drive to buy Indian spices in Sacramento, our meals turned mundane – meatloaf, pot roast, casseroles. They all tasted like apologies. Day by day, Amma's presence dimmed; she became a figure on pause.

At school, my teachers called me 'observant.' The word always came out with a slight edge, as if they meant something else. I watched my classmates with a mix of detachment and fascination – how they didn't appear to carry the weight of unsaid things on their shoulders, how their parents arrived to pick them up at precisely the same time each day, smiling easily. Normalcy looked foreign to me, like a language I could hear but not speak.

In spring, the almond blossoms returned in a sudden flush of pale petals. They fell past our windows in drifts of white confetti. Amma started going on long walks through the orchards while I was at school, returning with pollen caked on her sari hem. One evening I discovered her in Frankie's attic room, fingertips tracing the outline of the guitar case. She sensed me at the door. 'Some things,' she said softly in Tamil, 'are better left in their cases.' But I heard Frankie's name on her lips, too. It sounded out of place, caught between two languages.

When summer arrived and the valley turned scorching, the tule receded to the coastline. The unrelenting sun made every detail look harsh – each squeak of the floorboards, each crack along the walls. Appa spoke of other places – Chicago, New Jersey, Houston – cities with larger Indian communities, as though a fresh location could solve an unspoken ache. He repeated phrases like 'We'd fit better there.' He never said what was no longer fitting here.

Then, in August – eleven months to the day after Frankie first appeared – Amma vanished. I came home from summer school to find her passport gone, her wedding jewellry missing, the steel masala dabba set neatly on the kitchen counter as if waiting for someone else to claim it. A single note in careful English: 'Some songs need time to find their beginning.'

She'd taken Frankie's guitar case, too.

Appa and I lived in that house while the almonds ripened once more, mechanical shakers returning to rattle the branches like a collective lament. We fell into our own routines: microwave dinners on paper plates, passing one another in the hall like ships avoiding collision. On weekends, I sometimes climbed to the attic, just to stand in the dusty hollow where the guitar case had been, as if my presence might conjure Amma back.

This is what I say now: It was just another California year.

This is what I know: Time isn't measured by seasons or by the distance between Chennai and Sacramento. Some losses sprawl across a lifetime, uncontainable.

This is what remains: a house on Pine Ridge Road, a child's footprints on fifteen worn steps, a ghostly silhouette in attic dust, and the shape of a memory that never quite settles – like tule that hovers but refuses to touch the ground.

Eclipse

by Coral McCormack

Longlisted, Edinburgh Short Story Award 2025

For two-minutes-and-twenty-three-seconds at almost ten in the morning, day became night. *An eclipse of the sun*, static and faraway voices crackled through the islanders' radios. I sat on the hill to spectate, a box of odd paper glasses at my side, Mrs Murphy's cottage at my back, curtains drawn in anticipation. It was strange to be out in what should've been the sun hours, the sea heaving, breathing, hissing, pulling away from the shore – from *me*. Like the islanders.

The deer wrapped around my waist, head slumped over my knee, was still warm, its black eyes pinned on me. Accusing. With my stomach full, a liquid fatigue pouring over me, my eyes landed on a dark shape approaching on the horizon. A boat! Despite the satisfied heaviness anchoring me to the grass, my weak body begged for people. The animal catches and islander food weren't enough – I grew ravenous quickly, spiralling into such a state that I'd wake with blood smears over my face and no recollection of how they got there. Hunting animals wasn't my strong point, and so I raided cupboards, rationing pasta, beans, and potatoes, using Mrs Murphy's stove to cook them the same ways she had before I stuffed her.

If I craned my neck, I could see her waiting for me in the cottage, propped at the round table, her eyes permanently closed, a soft smile lifting her bulldog cheeks. It would've been unthinkable to have her staring at me the whole time. This way she looked pleased with my company, the way she used to. The other islanders were positioned in their clapboard houses, or their shops, frozen in the little scenes I'd choreographed. The baker stood at his till with floured hands; Joan leant over the railings at the docks, a can of beer in her hand – stuck with the glue I found at the post office – and cheeks blistered from saltwater. Stuffing them wasn't the craziest idea – fisherman Jim had a whole shelf dedicated to a collection of ugly animals. The fox was my favourite, but it was the eyes – the unblinking – they weren't *real*, and I needed Mrs Murphy and the others to look alive. Talking to an unblinking person was just as bad as talking to yourself. Had loneliness forced fisherman Jim to stuff the fox and birds? Had he mumbled to them over his puzzles the casual way I chatted to him now?

Deer blood dried and cracked on my chin. I spat out tufts of hair tickling the inside of my mouth. It was what I missed most about Mother: her mason jars of tepid blood stacked in the window of our hut in the woods, the smooth slide of it down my gullet. No lumps. No fur. When Mother vanished, it was Mrs Murphy who introduced me to their ways: rubbery roast chicken dinners, plate half-filled with greens, and endless hot chocolates to warm the devil's fingers rattling the windows. Mother's absence was now an imaginary friend of sorts – and just like Mrs Murphy and the others, I'd talk to it. And if I was talking to Mother's absence then at

160

least I wasn't talking to myself. It occurred to me once, when I found a dead fledgling on Mrs Murphy's doormat, caught in a slither of moonlight, that perhaps like birds, Mother wanted me to learn on my own, to kickstart some animalistic instinct within me by shoving me out of her nest.

With the island wrapped with towering evergreens, I entertained the thought that Mother was hiding somewhere in the forest, watching over me, examining what I'd do once her stockpile dwindled. The alternative didn't bear thinking about – that perhaps she had stepped out during the sun hours. What would happen exactly? The thought had crossed my mind as I'm sure it had Mother's. Books liked to describe the event as combusting into flames, limbs shrinking, throat shrieking, and whilst I had winced at that sharp sting of the sun, the backs of my eyelids blood-red, bright as a wound, Mother's vanishing wasn't preceded by wailing, nor the stink of scorched flesh, or thinning ribbons of smoke. She was just gone.

I never told Mrs Murphy – not even as I cradled her in my arms and observed the last swell of her chest – but my first feed without Mother's supply was Mrs Murphy's old cat, Ginger. Mrs Murphy had remained hopeful, pulling open the tabs of sardine tins and, leaving them out by the door, stood with the moon on her face, strange squeaking sounds on her lips. Guilt crystallised in my gut. It was the first time I felt regret. I'd done the decent thing and buried it while the island slept, but soon neighbours buzzed with stories of missing pets. Mrs Murphy repeated the theories to me as she basted chickens or chopped vegetables: a panther lurking in the woods, an alien phenomenon like the cow mutilations across the ranches in America in the seventies – though now they were abducting small pets. I shrank with each hypothesis, reminded of how different I was. The island was connected by shared histories of life here, but me and Mother were the misfits who hid away and scurried out at night like rats at the docks. Mother didn't care for them; the looks never bothered her. But I hated it – how a simple glance divided us. One group of girls who strutted into the public house every Friday night – faces bright with joy, sparkly blue eyelids, hair pulled tight, ponytails swishing, chokers around their necks, biceps bangled – were mesmerising to me. I'm ashamed to admit that out of the islanders, I fed on them first, part of me hoping I could absorb their lives for my own.

I clawed back the mole-like mound of soil by my feet and teased out a folded note. Pressing my lips together, I unfolded each layer and read the neat line of words. *I've seen you on the island – do you want to be friends? Write your answer on the back and cover it with the soil.* Every time I found one of the notes, my spirit lifted, my sight wobbling like the sea. But the happiness was fleeting; the writing was my own. I'd dotted more around the island: in the baker's till, in Joan's pocket, hidden in a crevice of a stone wall where a rock was missing. I even discussed the notes with Mrs Murphy when I returned to the cottage at dusk. Alone on the hill now, with the mocking *urrah, urrah, urrah* of the gannets, the sea breeze needled at my bones.

I shoved the deer away. It twisted, tumbling down the hill. With the back of my sleeve, I rubbed at the flaking blood until the cotton rusted. As the sun peeled around the moon, I spotted the boat and the soft shapes of people on the deck, could feel the rhythm of fresh pulses, the watery sound of blood gushing around their veins, could imagine their mouths forming words and laughter. My gaze lowered to the deer now caught against a boulder. The sun prickled my cheeks as I backed away, returning to the shade of the cottage. Mrs Murphy lay slumped over the table, cheek against the wood. I lifted her, positioning her back into place, limbs frozen, hand reaching for the cup of tea, an unsightly milk membrane floating on top, face the shade of sealskin.

Clotting inside me, was a hunger to transcend the limitations Mother set. *Alba, we are not to make friends. We are not like them.* I wanted to prove Mother wrong: if an ordinary existence wasn't meant for me then how could I crave it so? Perhaps I could change. It was a poetic justice of sorts – seeking to rid myself of this carnivorous compulsion having already purged the island of life. I observed the boat slice through the waves, my greed rumbling at the prospect of more islanders. I thumped at my stomach so hard it stung between my ribs. Once, in a gluttonous frenzy, Mrs Murphy devoured a whole plate of French Fancies, peeling back the fondant with her dentures for the smooth dome beneath, blaming it on her sweet tooth. Was that my problem? Did I have an insatiable blood tooth that needed the iron bitterness? If I could put myself on a diet like Mrs Murphy pretended to do week after week, I could live among new islanders. I could be like Martina – the vegan girl who always ordered tofu on her Friday nights out but then grimaced every time it passed her lips. With my back against the door, voices swept up the hill and whispered through the keyhole. The sad little note to myself crackled in my fist. And as my body buzzed with the newcomers piling onto the island, for all the moonlit conversations coming my way, for my last chance to be like them, the burning hunger both swelled and ebbed.

Jiggers

by Don J Taylor

Reader's Choice, Longlisted, Edinburgh Short Story Award 2025

If it hadn't been for King Charles' left eye, me and Jack would probably still be friends, I suppose. And things between me and Val...well, there might still *be* a me and Val.

We called ourselves The Joppa Jiggers, our little group, on account we all live in Joppa just outside Edinburgh, and we liked to get together, regular-like, to do jigsaws. We needed a name because we entered the odd quiz at the Ship Inn too, and then there were regional jigsaw team competitions. When I first suggested the name, Norma – that's Jack's wife – complained.

'Google says jiggers are revolting tropical sand fleas that burrow into your flesh,' she said.

Then Jack said, 'Sand fleas be damned, it's the measure I use to make our cocktails.' He had several jiggers in his 'Sanctuarium Subterraneum' – that's the bar he built in his basement. So, if Jack approved, and my wife Val would never dare contradict him, then 'Joppa Jiggers' it was. You could say that Jack, Norma, Val and me were interlocked.

On one of our Friday evenings we warmed up with *The Young Squire Comes of Age*. Jack called it an 'amuse bouche' (he was always full of BS) in advance of the night's main course, which, he promised, was 'something special I picked up on my travels'.

The Squire, as we called it, was a 388-piece wavy-edged picture. Released in the nineteen forties, I think, but it's set in the seventeen hundreds, with the local folk sat round a long table in the garden of a country mansion. The old Squire (I've got him down as a widower) is presenting his son to the retainers – those he will lord it over in due course. There are matronly ladies, farm managers in pork-pie hats, and peasants in their smocks; all smiles and enjoying the Squire's bounty. It's one of my favourites. I like the little dramas in the picture: the serving girl with the pitcher of cider who's only got eyes for the handsome young footman; the young bucks watching the heir-apparent with looks that say 'get *him*!'; the older lady behind the old Squire with a faraway look in her eye, like she's imagining what might have been if the Squire hadn't married her cousin from the next parish. It makes it all rather interesting, and putting together the pieces focuses your attention on what's really going on in the picture. But the look on that lady's face brought to mind how, every now and then that summer, I would catch Val sitting in the conservatory staring into space. 'That'll be the menopause', I thought to myself. I said nothing, though. Well, it's not for a husband to pry into that sort of thing, is it?

As usual, that Friday, we were in the aforementioned *sanctuarium*. It smells of damp on account of the walls are exposed brick, and with such a low ceiling I have to walk around like a half-shut knife, unlike Jack who's a podgy short-arse. We had just packed away *The Squire* when Jack drags out a large folding table. He flips down the legs and planks it in front of us. 'We need a big space for my next offering,' he announces. 'I picked it up in Valladolid.'

I caught Norma giving an eye-roll, which drew a sharp look from Val. Jack never tired of retelling tales of his trip to the International Jigsaw championships in Spain. He was placed 36th in the individual competitions, with a time of one hour thirty-six for a 500-piecer. Not bad really, I have to admit. The completed framed jigsaw had pride of place in the basement, hanging next to his certificate.

In a little room off the main space he kept his 'adult puzzles'. Like a Victorian gent might keep his risqué art works slightly apart: titles like *Topless Brunettes at the Lido, Naughty Christmas at St Trinians,* or *Betty Boop's Slutty Sister.* Quite a contrast to the normal fare of *The Old Sweet Shop, Autumn in Paris,* or *Cutty Sark Close-Hauled and Homeward Bound.*

Jack emptied the contents of a large cardboard box onto the table.

'One thousand little beauties,' he said. 'Think we're up to it?'

He propped the box lid up against the cocktail shaker, so we could see the picture. Well, *Jack* could see it alright. Val sat opposite Jack, and I was facing Norma, so we three were all kind of craning to get a good look. The picture was a portrait (by Daniël Mijtens, it said on the box) of King Charles – not the current king, but Charles I, the one that got his head chopped off. He's looking over his left shoulder towards the viewer, gloved hand on hip, just above his sword hilt. The sky is painted a silvery grey, echoing the silky sheen of his shirt. That's the problem with paintings – historical ones anyway – artists like to link in the colour schemes from the main subject into the background. A nightmare for us dissectologists. Dissectologists – that's the posh name for jigsaw fans.

Norma served snacks ('Tapas' Jack called them) while Jack opened a bottle of red for Norma, then poured Mojitos for the rest of us. It was a warm evening so the ladies were in summer dresses. Jack was sockless in plum-coloured shorts, below a garish orange and green shirt. I stuck to my usual plain grey T-shirt and M & S chinos. Jack spread out the pieces and we started turning them picture-side up. Jack said to me, 'You take the sky, Gordon. In Spain we found it's better to divvy up the areas. You'll be good on sky. I'll take the head and the hat, they're quite tricky. Let's try timing this one, folks. What do you think – just to give ourselves an idea of what we might do in a competition? Agreed?' And he tapped the stopwatch on his iPhone.

I said nothing, but married up a bunch of dark green leaves with a fluffy cloud and pressed it in with a little click. I'd learned there was no point in taking Jack on head to head.

The table fell silent as we worked through the puzzle. It was rather a nice picture. We had all the edges in place, obviously, and were getting to that stage where everything was falling into place, the point when, no matter how seasoned you are, you can't help getting just a little excited. I noticed that Val, in particular, had a dreamy smile on her lips and was swaying gently, but rhythmically, in her chair.

'You know what,' said Jack, his hands slotting pieces into place almost on auto-pilot, all the while checking his phone. (He prided himself on being a 'multi-tasker') 'We're heading for not a bad time on this one, keep it up guys. How's that walking cane coming on, Val?' he asked with just the hint of a smirk.

'Oh I feel it's coming on just fine,' she said, a little breathlessly; almost *panting*, you might say.

'You on track with the sky, Gordon?' Jack asked in that condescending tone he favoured.

'There, I'm done,' I said pressing the last bit of grey into place.

'Who's got the left eye?' demanded Jack, looking directly across the table at Val.

Everyone scanned the table, but there was no eye. I shifted my foot and felt something slide beneath my sole on the tiled floor. I held my counsel, but ducked my head beneath the table to retrieve what must be the king's eye.

It was like that moment when you glimpse a mouse scurrying across the garage floor. You *see* it, and at the same time you *don't*. I'll never forget Jack's right leg jerking back like it was spring-loaded, bare foot scrabbling for his loafer; and Val's legs snapping together, frantic fingers tugging her dress back down over her knees. I resurfaced from the sub-table underworld. Val fidgeted with her wedding ring, her face beetroot red, while Jack fussed with the timer on his phone. Norma calmly carried on necking her usual quota of Argentine Malbec.

'The final piece!' I announced calm as you like, and slotted the King's eye into place to complete the picture.

Then, grasping the table-edge, I up-ended the whole caboodle. Up went King Charles, left eye and all! I swept clear the tables, set along the walls, spread with half-finished puzzles. Then I started on the boxes shelved in ascending order of size, 300 up to 2000; next, the soft porn from the private passageway, smashing the frames and sending pouting lips, mascaraed eyelashes, and pert nipples whirling across the room like autumn leaves in a hurricane. Jack sat stupefied, as *Cotswold Cottages* mingled with *Spring in an Alpine Meadow*; *Pyramids and Sphinx* jumbled with *Sunset on the Serengeti,* and *Art Treasures of the Vatican* mashed-up with *Where's Wally on Brighton Beach.*

Val shrieked at me – 'Jack, have you taken leave of your senses?'

'Not in the least,' I replied, with a smile that reflected my deep, deep sense of fulfilment. 'It's long overdue, and I'm *totally* fine.'

'Good for you!' slurred Norma. 'The bassard had it comin', and she grabbed *Apollo 11 Moon Landing* from my grasp. With a whoop of joy she sent six hundred pieces of grey lunar landscape flying across the room. The floor was inches deep in twenty thousand irregular shapes that could never, ever, in a million years, be reassembled. Norma's grand gesture threw her off balance and she tipped off the chair onto the floor.

'Come on Norma,' I said, helping her to her feet. 'Stay at ours tonight. I mean *mine*. Val won't be coming home any time soon. In fact, *ever*. Do *you* darling?' I asked, looking at my soon-to-be-ex wife. She slumped her cradled head onto a car-crash amalgam of *When did You Last See your Father* and *Sultry Shanghai Girls*.

I heard later at the Ship Inn that Val moved in with her sister in Trinity. Jack and Norma split up. He sold up his share in his legal firm to buy a villa in the Algarve. Six months later Kaarina from Finland, a competitor he'd met at Valladolid, joined him. Nobody in 'The Ship' knew anything about Norma.

The one thing the whole sorry saga taught me is that the beauty of jigsaws – and I'm now in a new group in Portobello called Porty Puzzle Partners – is that they really make you look hard at what's in front of you; you notice things you might not clock in the normal way of seeing things.

Old Penny Peat

by Abby Walker

Longlisted, Edinburgh Short Story Award 2025

Granda had been waiting for me the last time I was here, sat on the low stone wall in the yard with his shirt off. Wiry up top, the skin sagging from his bones like damp kitchen roll, grey curls thinning on his chest. A distended belly below it, painful and homely, resting on his legs. He was staring at the air, utterly still, his expression relaxed into a decades-old scowl that I knew he didn't feel.

I've always found it fascinating about him, the way he can wait. No need to occupy his time, no need for distraction, no sign of agitation. The ability, simply, to sit and wait.

Nana was crouched next to me beside the kitchen window, cleaning one of the cupboards. Tupperware piled on the countertop, organised in size order. Her lap was full of assorted lids.

'He's due a cut again,' she said. 'And do his back, too.'

Nana's back in the cupboards – the pan one this time. She's trying to fit each one inside another, finding the order in which they can all be tucked away. She holds a saucepan in one hand, hovers it over the others like a divining rod, then sucks her teeth and lets it clang to the floor.

'Put that in the bin, will you.'

I pick it up instinctively then put it down. This isn't why I'm here.

'Where is he?'

Nana shakes her head, muttering as she picks up a frying pan.

'Nana.'

'No good.' She hands me the pan and I put it down with the other.

'Where's Granda?'

'Haven't seen him since breakfast. Went up, got washed, came down, he was gone.'

She glances up at me. 'I'm not his carer, pet. And he doesn't need one.'

'I just need to talk to him.'

'Don't go bringing it up.'

'I won't.'

A lie. Nana sees it and nods, resigned.

'Our Alex might know. He's been staying since Thursday.'

I find my cousin, alone, by the banana factory wall, where I knew he would be. His football thuds off the wall and returns to him, and he leans in to observe the ground. It was a game I used to play when I was younger too. A strong kick of a ball against the stone wall on a warm day bringing out a trickle of brightly coloured spiders through the cracks. Some are thick-bodied, others spindly, all of them glimmering with the sweat of a long journey, the skittering agitation of waking in a place that doesn't smell like home.

Yellow ones are worth 10 points. Bodies bigger than a 10p get 30. Whoever's kick unearths the spider that gets the biggest reaction gets a bonus 50. This is harder to achieve when playing alone.

Alex swings his leg back and pounds the football against the wall. It lands with a dull thunk. He needs a new one.

'You winning?'

He turns.

There used to be a time when seeing me would send him into hysterics, jumping up into my arms with his full weight and momentum. Now his face clouds as he kicks the ball again, his dismissal permission for me to come to him. There are lots of new languages to be learnt, ones I don't remember using at his age.

'What d'you want?' he mumbles.

'Granda,' I say. 'Seen him?'

Alex kicks at the ground with the heel of his trainers.

'Behave, you'll scuff them.'

'I haven't seen him."

"You know why I wanna see him.'

'Yeah.'

'You friends with the kid?'

'Not anymore. His mam says I'm not allowed to knock for him.'

'You see it happen?' I say.

'A bit.'

'And?'

Alex shrugs.

'Alex. Did he hit him?'

'Just grabbed him. It was just the way Granda went running in, made it look more.

He just pulled him out.'

'How did he pull him?'

'By his shirt.'

'Not by the neck?'

Alex shrugs, dropping his eyes again.

'And when he grabbed the kid. Did he hold him under the water?'

'He maybe fell a bit,' Alex says. 'He's not good on his feet.'

'Yeah, I know.'

Alex kicks the ball and a small orange spider darts from between the mortar, disappearing into the stones.

It won't be long for you, I want to tell him. *This place will be behind you soon.*

'I think that's a 10,' I say.

Alex kicks again. I wait to see if he will offer me the ball. He doesn't.

He could be fishing, but I know he's not. He gave it up after Uncle Carl, when he got in his head. I'd been walking to the house from the bottom of the terrace where I'd parked when I saw the little kid at number four, playing in her Wendy house in the front yard. From the gables of the wooden house was a sign hung with fishing wire, scribbled in whiteboard marker: SHOP OPEN TODAY. Around the sign were red and blue fishing lures, dangling from the roof like Christmas ornaments.

When I'd gotten to the house, the limp tongues of Granda's waders were drooping out of the bin lid. Nana rescued them when I told her, rolling her eyes and saying he was 'on one', that he'd regret giving it all away when whatever idea he had gotten into his head faded.

He is not fishing, but he is at the river. Old habits.

'Granda.'

He begins to turn and I quicken my steps to come to his side before he has to stand from the chair.

'What you doing here?' I ask.

'Sitting,' he says.

He settles back into the camp chair, facing the river.

'Not fishing?'

'Nope,' he says, simply, defiantly, like he knows why I'm asking.

'Can I sit with you?'

'Suit yourself.'

I sit on the bank beside his chair, the earth baked dry. I run my fingers over the cracks, dig my nails into it, like I used to as a child when I watched him fish. He would bring me a tin of sardines for dinner, tell me to eat them with my back turned to the river, so as not to intimidate the fish.

'Now don't you start,' he says.

'I haven't even said anything.'

'You're thinking.'

'I'm reminiscing,' I say and hear his sardonicism in my voice.

A silence passes between us. The river flows slow enough to seem frozen, its surface pitted only with skating flies. The bare sun glows through the peat in the water and brings up the rust of old childhood. It's moving lower in the sky, almost at the crenelations of the churchyard yon side of the river. The church will be empty, as it is most of the time. I don't remember ever seeing anyone visiting outside of christenings or funerals.

When I was little, I used to pretend to see people in the stained glass windows.

She's waving at you, Granda, I would say. And he would say *is she now?* and I would say yes and it would feel like secret and important, this world only I could access, of my own making. Sometimes I would believe it so deeply, build it so strong in my mind that it would become too big for me, those waving hands too sharp in their silhouettes, and I would start to cry.

Keep on with that, Granda would say. *And a big old catfish'll smell that salt on your face and jump right out of the water to lick it up.*

And the thought of a catfish in our little river would make me laugh and it would be forgotten.

'What happened, Granda?'

I expect him to snap, but he doesn't. He's silent, and I don't dare look at him, don't dare move, don't dare spook him. *Just hold nice and still now.*

'It's the river,' he says. 'The laddie was in, and he shouldn't have been.'

'Why shouldn't he have been?'

'It's not safe.'

'I used to play in there. You used to play in there with me.'

'It's changing.'

Granda's voice is soft, and I know I must wait again for him.

'Do you think of home when you're gone?' he says.

'I think of you,' I tell him.

'You all can think of us when you're gone, but you don't think of it.'

He nods to the river. Then he points at the cemetery, to the stained glass windows of my imaginary worlds.

'They're leaving too.'

His finger trembles. He rests it back on his knee.

'It's more than peat making it dark,' he says.

Something sinks in me, something soft and hard to grasp or stop. Its pain is not sharp; now it's here, it feels inevitable.

'Why would the people in the cemetery leave?' I ask lightly.

'They don't have a choice in it.'

'Oh.'

'Not like you didn't have a choice, because you did,' he says, without venom. 'We've all got a choice till we end up in there.'

He nods across the river, at the headstones that seem suddenly closer to the bank than I remember them.

'The ground's giving them up.'

'Why would it do that?'

Granda takes a deep breath. There is something in it, not a rattle or a wheeze, but a heaviness, the presence of something.

'It'd rather be alone than abandoned.'

I want him to look at me. I can't look at the side of his face anymore. I want to see his eyes and to hold him, even though we haven't held each other for a long time now. I know he can feel it, how much I want it, but he does not turn to me.

One side of his mouth ticks up.

'You think I've gone barmy.'

'No.'

'I can hear it in your voice.'

I stop myself from denying it. I can hear it, too.

I stand up. The sun is low now, catching the red in the river, reflecting the bronze

hue of old-penny peat into Granda's face.

'Let's go back to the house, Granda.'

But he is still. A stillness of something old and immovable.

'I think I'll wait here, kidda,' he says, and I sit myself back at his feet.

Footprints

by Cara Watson

Longlisted, Edinburgh Short Story Award 2025

1587
Ardmore Bay, Isle of Skye

Tis' almost nightfall.

There is a thick layer of mist suffocating most of the land.
Tis' getting dark and cald. The hair on my arms reaches
out into the quickly darkening fog around me. And so I
pull on my shawl a little tighter this eve, and I follow the
rest of my herd towards the chapel. Tis' snowing, tis'
been snowing for weeks. The journey to the chapel feels
longer at nighttime. It's miles away from our village.
Miles away from anything.

Our church wobbles on the edge of a high cliff above the
North Sea. A small stumble would send you plummeting
to your death on the rocky bay below. So we make sure to
stay close to one another and always keep a few metres
back from the edge. When you can.

Do you feel that? There's such a caldness coming in from
the sea tonight. It's blowing through Lassie's skirts,
making us wish we were men. Making us wish and wish
on.

Quicker now, I follow the dotted line of amber lanterns
over the snow. Footprints falling on top of footprints.
Disappearing a few moments later under new

snowflakes.

Here, and then gone.

The village is praying. Praying for a brighter future. Praying for a future at all.

I sneak one last look at the misty, white grounds, but we dinnae stay out there for long. We pile into the auld chapel. The heavy wooden doors are urged shut by the wind, and then mutterings fall into hushed silence. My wee brother is beside me. I hold his hand in mine. I think that he's made of snowflakes now. I plant a kiss on his palm and hold it tighter. I lead us through the shivering crowd into a corner, by a window that needs fixing. The wind creeps in, slicing and skinning the living.

Tis' loud in the chapel and we can barely hear our minister rattling on from his step.

I tell my brother to close his eyes and pray for the spirit of our father.

For the spirit of our mother. For our spirits not yet taken. I tell him to pray.

Pray for a brighter future, I say. Pray for a future at all.

And then I begin my own prayer.

I ask the lord to have mercy, to save my wee brother's heart from freezing to death.

I ask the lord over and over. I plead with him, I do. *Please. Please.*

I hope he can't hear the thing that's lingering under my prayers.

A place within me still spits and crackles for the sacrifice of our mother and father. For the hardship we have faced since. For the guilt I have felt, for the cursing, for the questioning of God's intentions. The guilt is heavy, but there's something else, something stronger, something seething.

I open my eyes in fear that someone is listening.
But everybody is too busy with their own prayers.
Soft murmurs and weeping mothers fill every nook and cranny.
At least there's hope here… if that's what it is.

Suddenly, I feel the wind retreat from the broken window beside me.
My whole body is shivering. Tis' ice. Almost ice.
I pull my auld shawl further around me, tis' like a mother's firm embrace.
I peer through the crack in the window.

And as I do, my heart stops.
My whole body braces. My feet become stone.
I stop breathing.
I stop blinking.
I am as still as a deer is when it catches its hunter's eye.

The night outside is too calm, too quiet.
I peer further through the window, further into the night.
I swear I see something… out there… moving through the misty snowfall.

It can't be…

In a split second, my brother's small hand melts away from mine.
I move closer to the window.
The moon, like a lantern, points its pale finger.
A familiar face looks back at me. I must be dreaming. Or freezing.
Because as I watch him, he watches me the same.

Tis' my father, my dead father.

I open my mouth to scream… to weep… to pray…
But just as I do, a dark and woody scent crawls into my
mouth, down my throat and up my nostrils.
My eyes circle the chapel, and the smell grows stronger.
I become a hawk as I seek. I stop my search at the door.
A small figure stands on tiptoes, peering outside through
a gap of splintered wood.
And before I realise it's smoke covering his face, I watch
him turn to me and whisper,

Papa.

The whole chapel lights up like the lord has sent bright
angels to our door.
But these angels are glowing red, and the smell of
burning grows and grows.
It isn't just wood we're smelling now.

I throw myself to the door, but it's too hard to see
anything. The room is black with smoke. I see flashes of
white claws and wide eyes as folk try to find a way out. I
shout my brother's name, and I grasp the small spaces I
can find in front of me, hoping he'll come running into
my arms. But he doesn't… and I can't breathe.
Something makes me think that this was no accident. Not
with all the troubles of land envy. We are being attacked.
They're here…

Time is running out. I cry out for my brother, again and
again and again. I promise, I do. But he does not come.
He does not come.

And then I think of the small broken window that
showed me my father's ghostly watch. And I force myself

through the burning and the smoke. I force myself through the fallen figures and collapsing lungs that take their last creak of breath in this world.

And like a deer springs over a fallen tree, I throw myself through the small gap in the window. The hot and broken glass slices across my chest and pierces through muscle, but I don't have the breath to scream. The icy night blanket welcomes me like an ally and soothes my burns and cuts. And so I run. I run over snow, through snow, across the ice. I run from the blazing church behind me, and into the dark cald night. My thighs greet a new burn, as my muscles splinter with every step. I run back through the snowed-over trail which led us here, only moments before.

How much a night can change in these parts?

Suddenly, I hate the land I grew up on. I hate the men that fight over it.
This stupid, deathly land.
There's blood dripping onto the white snow. My blood?
I realise that I'm creating a trail.
If the snow doesn't cover it in time…
They'll catch me.

But I don't stop.

Time passes strangely from now on.
Perhaps it's the bite of the cald night,
or the open wound bleeding out onto it.
Maybe something else is at hand,
something in the air, or the past that the land is made up of.

But something lifts me and carries me further.
I look down at my feet. Tis' my two feet.
Tis' my bleeding body. Tis' me.

Eleven miles I will run.
Eleven miles I will bleed.
Eleven miles I will haunt.

But I'm almost there.
Even if this land is doomed, I'll fight till death to protect
it. My bloody bond, my downfall. My love for my land.
My hate for my land.

I'll burn with it if I must.
But I have to try.

I don't think of them.
Of my family.
I try so hard not to think of them.
My wee brother.
I pray he got out.
And when hope goes, I will surrender.
But not until I ring the bell.

The village is in sight now.
It looks so quiet, so calm.
I can hear them catching up with me,
fire will catch if I'm not fast enough.

And so I use the last breath left in me.
The breath I have been saving the entirety of my wee life.
And I start to scream. I scream from my guts.

THEY'RE COMING! THEY'RE COMING!

Folk will be stirring now, from their evening duties.
The elder folk, the sick folk that didnae make it to the chapel.
They'll all be rising.
Why should they be damned just because of their weakness?
They are just as worthy as anyone else.
They deserve to live.

The last push.
I throw my torn up body into the air and I grab onto the rope of the bell.
And I ring it until my hands become part of it. Until I am one with the bell.
I don't stop.
I feel my body starting to shut down, but I fight it.
My clothes are soaking from my sweat and blood.
But I fight it.
My hands become locked in position.
I'll die this way.

There's plenty of commotion outside now.
Not sure I saved anybody.
But I allow myself to hope.
As I feel my body begin to give in, I hope for a brighter future. For a future at all.
For a future worth living, where folk dinnae slaughter each other for land.
It will come, *i hope.* It will come.
One day, they'll be free.
My mother, my father. My wee brother.
And ae'body's children, and their children, and theirs.
They'll be free.

The bell rings.

At first, there's a ringing…
One, two, three, minutes of it…
It's in my ears, it's buzzing from the floor beneath me,
and right through my body.

Echoes of my voice susurrate around me…
Echoing now, echoing still…
In the blood drops. In the footprints under snowfall.

Here… and then gone.

*This is a story based on truth. The Battle of the Spoiling Dyke, when
one young woman ran eleven miles to warn her clan of an attack.
The woman's name is unknown.*

Edinburgh Flash Fiction Awards 2025

First Prize
Cecilia Maddison, *Wild Horses*

Second Prize
Alexandra Lane, *The Great Ivories*

Third Prize
Judith Allnatt, *War Bride*

Golden Hare Award
Margaret McMillan, *Homesickly*

Write Mango Flash Award
Katy Hughes, *Swansong*

Highly Commended
Sahara De Ville, *Press '2' to Save*
Katharine Powlett, *Wear your Pink Coat*
Titash Sen, *Postal Child*
Alexis Somerville, *Miniature Love Story*

Editor's Choice
Robert Tateson, *One Horse Town*

Wild Horses

by Cecilia Maddison

Winner, Edinburgh Flash Fiction Award 2025

'Weather's changing,' said Mam at the window, her sharp eyes skinning the mackerel sky. She stirred figures of eight in the oxtail stew, her mouth a cross-stitched seam.

I gathered cotton and clouds from the washing line. The little ones clung to my hem like burrs when I folded the sheets, laying them straight and snapping them flat. Mary watched from her fireside bed, her eyes brimming green, for with every high tide the sea poured in and pooled where her breath belonged.

The Priest came by to bow his head, his moth-hands fluttering the sign of the cross. His black coat billowed when he bade farewell as if to take flight with the crows.

'They're close now,' Mary called after him, 'galloping over the waves.' Her face shone, slick with sweat and holy water, and Mam bolted the door.

Around the weary, grained table we supped, our faces bobbing like moons on water and the silver spoons slipping fish-quick to and from our lips. Only Mary's place was empty for she wilted on her pillow, and her chest heaved tunes we didn't care for.

I heard them in the night, those horses with thundering hooves, and I felt their foaming breath on my cheek. By morning Mary was far away on the back of them, with only her ragdoll body left behind. God forgive me but the thought of her soul blazing as they charged across the horizon made my heart leap like raindrops on the barn roof.

The Great Ivories

by Alexandra Lane

Second Prize, Edinburgh Flash Fiction Award 2025

They say there's a new show in the city, one that no well-bred lady or gentleman should miss. They say Arctic explorers stumbled across a tusk larger than any ever found, protruding out of the melting permafrost, and only discovered that the fully preserved bull mammoth it was attached to was alive when it began to defrost. What did they do with it? They carved keys right into those great tusks and coupled it to some massive musical contraption in the old opera house. They sat two young ladies in virginal white before that colossus, one at each tusk, and had them play.

They say the music is so pure it causes the mammoth to weep. Broadsides and hawkers alike claim one crystal vial of 'Titan's Tears' will cure what ails you, never mind the price.

And when he dies at last, when his bones are all that remains, the mark of us will still be cut deep into those great ivories; they will sit gathering dust in a palace-sized cabinet of curiosities, amidst the yellowed bones of his brethren.

They say the moths have changed from white to something darker because the trees are darker now too and this is how they must survive us and our black pall of smoke; and I have a feeling, a feeling the great titan is not crying for itself, and that maybe we should count ourselves lucky we've lost only this much.

War Bride

by Judith Allnatt

Third Prize, Edinburgh Flash Fiction Award 2025

Her wedding gown is made from parachute silk – the same parachute that saved him. At the hospital, he told her how he'd jumped from the burning plane, plummeted, jerked stiff as a tin soldier as the 'chute opened and slowed as it billowed above him. In the half-light, the smell of lavender rose to meet him from the fields before he could see the spread of blue. Over the noise of the wind that pummelled his ears, he heard the whine as the plane went down, Tom trapped in the cockpit. It hit the ground far below him to the west and opened like a rose then smudged in a plume of black smoke. He held tight to the straps, dangling, helpless.

In the room at the boarding house, the dress, thrown off as soon as they were alone, lies across a chair in a crumple of creamy white. There is a trace of lavender in the scent of the sheets and when they make love he weeps, unable to feel blessed. All night, through the buffeting of his dreams he holds tight to her hand – his parachute girl – while she lies awake, wondering if she can bear the weight of his war.

Homesickly

by Margaret McMillan

Winner, Golden Hare Award for Scottish Flash Fiction 2025

Gary in Bay 3 is snoring, visible only as a mound under crumpled white sheets stamped in red: 'NHS Property'.

Prof frowns. Shit, I left out Gary's postcode from my summary of his case. In Prof's mind, every postcode has its evils. If Gary came from Knightsbridge he'd be vulnerable to expense accounts at Harrods.

 But he doesn't.

'Rough sleeper,' I say. Glaswegian like me, I don't say.

Prof turns with a triumphant smile to the medical students on the ward round.

 'Encapsulates the issues. Poverty… substance misuse…'

He pulls back the top sheet. Gary is in a hospital gown, well, almost. Pulled over his forehead is a gunmetal grey bunnet. Below it, his nose has the texture of a blackberry and the colour of a rosehip.

 'Gettaefuck,' he roars. You see them hunched round Euston like a Greek chorus telling fresh migrants from Glasgow that the streets of London arenae paved with fuckin' gold. Migrants like me.

Prof shakes Gary's shoulder. 'I'm Professor Fox.'

 Gary groans, eyes tight shut.
'Ahdoantcareifyoureprofessor-fuckinantelope.' His

196

stubble glints ginger as he rolls over, arse-to-Prof. Prof recoils, an anti-fart reflex I wish I'd learnt at medical school.

'I'm sensing disengagement here,' he says. 'Where's the Scottish girl?' He catches my eye. 'Yes, you.'

I've worked for him for three months and he knows me by my vowels.

'Talk to this man.' He moves to Bay 4, while Gary and I talk the English of the dispossessed. We don't belong here. It's time we went home.

Swansong

by Katy Hughes

Winner, Write Mango Flash Award 2025

First stop and search was Yusuf. Walking home from
football, hoody on, suspicious behaviour. Then Danny,
'loitering', then German Luke, no reason given. German
Luke's in our German class; there's Saturday Luke too,
works in Tescos on Saturdays and lets us buy vapes, but
no-one stops and searches ginger kids.

After that we thought fuck it, if they want criminals we
can do that. Adi robbed a kilo box of crisps from the
corner shop, Jameel tagged every lamppost on the block.
They weren't caught, but when it was their turn to be
pushed against the wall, patted down, at least they knew
inside there was something.

Then me. Pinned in place, hands on my body, bag
emptied out. My turn to give them a reason. No pussy
pilfering from the shop, a proper reason.

It weren't easy, and I'm the only one who got caught, but
it's worth every bit of shit that comes down on me. Piracy
on the high seas. Put that on my record.

Easy getting the padlock off, not easy getting it in the sea.
And twelve miles out is no joke, no idea which way
you're going in the dark, but I just pointed the beak of
that pedalo swan at the moon and prayed Google Maps
would keep working. Never been so scared or so
exhausted. Coastguard picked me up soon as I stopped

pedalling, hiding out there with their engine and lights off waiting for boats coming the other way.

Press '2' to Save

by Sahara De Ville

Highly Commended, Edinburgh Flash Fiction Award 2025

I know the end looms near, because I've started saving
my mother-in-law's voice messages. It's not that we've
always been close. Through the phone, she crackles and
wavers, her breath more laboured than before. I *feel* her
effort in my bones, *hear* the weariness lacing each
perfectly rounded vowel she produces. She was an
English teacher, after all. Her pauses linger longer than
they used to, I note as I lean in listening, assessing. '...*Bye,
then!*' Gone is the autopilot reaction of pressing '*3 to
delete.*' By selecting '*2 to save message*', I'm tucking them
away for safekeeping, into my phone's filing cabinet of
memory, and, behind my breast. Even the most mundane
message now stays.

She calls to say she's tired of being tired, that none of the
medications work. She doesn't recommend getting old, as
if I can somehow avoid it. The closer she shuffles towards
death upon swollen ankles, the preciousness of her words
grow. She spits syllables of saffron and sapphire. No
longer acidic critique. Coughs and sputters? *Keep*. Tell me
about the complex lives of random neighbours I never
met and never will. Say those shocking things that once
made me blush peony pink. The stories I heard a
hundred times, tell me a thousand times more. I want to
capture her smiling sounds, for when my heart is heavy

with missing her, I'll press my phone hard against my ear
till it hurts and keep her breathing, still.

Wear your Pink Coat

by Katherine Powlett

Highly Commended, Edinburgh Flash Fiction Award 2025

'Wear your pink coat,' he rasps.

'Why?' I ask, trying to sound as if any of this is normal.

'You'll stand out more.'

I pull it on and let the fur collar brush my cheek.

His look is intense, absorbing the essence of me, and I want to sink into those dark welling eyes. They hold two decades of our lives.

'Don't cry.' His quiet voice cracks.

Hot tears press and my throat aches. He pulls me in and wraps his once bear-hug arms around me. I'm calmed by his peaty tobacco smell.

'It's time,' he says.

'I don't want to go.'

'Me neither.' Joking to the last, he glances at the vial he'd bought from the dark web.

I linger on the threshold, by the newly installed video doorbell, yearning to reverse time. I mask my trembling lips with clashing red lipstick. In the corner shop, I remember to chat and eye the CCTV as I pay for the tissues. Jittery at the communal table in the library, I leaf through the newspapers without reading. A librarian in a Christmas jumper asks if I'm alright.

My phone lights up announcing 'Doorbell' and I scurry into the street.

'I'm responding to a call from this address?' says the police officer, grainy on my screen.

'I'm not there. I can buzz you in.'

My legs buckle but must carry me back to my hollowed-out home. Wind blows the tears from my eyes and I'm glad of the pink coat.

Postal Child

by Titash Sen

Highly Commended, Edinburgh Flash Fiction Award 2025

My mother wanted to send my father a message. So, she thought it best to put me in an old duffel bag with my head sticking out. She stitched five annas worth of stamps on my coat sleeves and stuck me in the post.

The postman looked at my scrawny shape and rickety legs and tskd. He hoisted me, duffel and all, onto his back and cut me a slice of raw mango with chilli powder as we went about his daily round. Enjoy this, he said, there are no mangoes in London. I took it, wondering why my mother would send me to a place devoid of mangoes. He must be wrong.

The postmaster had an angry face with big round eyes. His eyebrows came together, caterpillar-like, in a pronounced frown as he stuck a paper with instructions on my forehead.

They put me in a giant sack of letters that smelled like ink and unsaid things. There was a long dark. I thought I could no longer see.

When I saw light again – a new postmaster, smart of dress, smelling clean, with pale skin like the moon. He saw me. But also, didn't see I was a child.

An impatient postman lifted me far too easily and deposited me on my father's doorstep that cold and foggy morning.

I did not know how to read. But buried among the unsaid things, my mother's words had materialised on my now papery skin, printed in sooty black letters.

Miniature Love Story

by Alexis Somerville

Highly Commended, Edinburgh Flash Fiction Award 2025

He was so tiny on her wrist that people on the metro never noticed him, until today. He got through the barrier without a ticket of course, coasting on hers. And it wasn't like he didn't appreciate it. Sometimes he longed for their roles to be reversed so he could do more for her, or at least for them to inhabit the same world so they could achieve some kind of balance. But mostly he was just grateful to have met her. This stunning giantess who always listened to him, no matter how hard she had to strain her ears.

'What's that you got there?' A gargantuan finger pushed up against the back of his head.

'Get your grubby hands off him! That's my boyfriend.'

The older woman wore a teal shellsuit and shiny pink visor. Her own watch was a Casio, not a boyfriend. She was probably just jealous.

'Doesn't seem right, pretty young lady like you.'

'All my friends say he looks like a handsome K-pop star, so I'm not sure I get your point.'

'Well, does he have a job?'

The younger woman stroked her boyfriend's hair and held him up to the window. They took in the reflections of the carriage, the stuffy black air. 'I'm okay,' he said, just loud enough for her to hear over the rush of the train. Anyway, he had a job lined up for the summer, at the model village. They'd be lucky to have him.

One Horse Town

by Robert Tateson

Editor's Choice, Shortlisted, Edinburgh Flash Fiction Award
Shortlisted Write Mango Award 2025

Robbing the Littleton Bank was easy, it was escaping that gave Jake and me the problems; our horse, Josephine, was from Quebec and only understood French.

After we'd tied up the bank teller (he was also the manager) and grabbed the dollar bills, Jake leaped onto the driving seat of our buckboard and yelled, 'Yeeeehaaar!'

Josephine didn't budge.

Jake cracked the reins 'Walk on! Giddy-up! Please!'

Josephine turned her head and gave Jake a haughty Gallic stare.

I grabbed the reins, 'Allez!' She still refused to move. Then I realised that Jake had already blown it. If you enter an incorrect password three times, the horse locks you out. I tried 'allez!', 'ALLEZ!' and even '!alLez' but it was hopeless.

'We need an expert.'

We rushed into The Littleton Saloon, 'Is there a horse whisperer in town?' The bartender raised his hand.

'You the horse whisperer and the barman?'

He nodded.

'We're locked out of our horse. Help.' I pleaded, offering him a fistfull of dollars.

He shook his head.

'Why?'

He wrote on a notepad: *Lost my voice.*

'Not even a whisper?'

Headshake. *Try telegram to Houston Horse-Tech for a one-time reset password.*

'Where's the Telegraph Office?'

Turn left, 3rd door.

We charged into the office. I grabbed a form and scribbled: JUST ROBBED BANK STOP HORSE WONT START STOP and pushed it over the counter.

'Well that's mighty interesting, boys,' the clerk drawled, fingering his sheriff's star.

That's the trouble with one horse towns, everyone has two jobs.

Home

by Maria Saba

Shortlisted, Edinburgh Flash Fiction Award 2025

Home is the scent of moist soil in a hot summer afternoon; the first poem she learned as a child: ما گل های خندانیم   فرزندان ایرانیم; the deer in the meadow on her grandmother's handmade carpet; the red cherry stains on her white shirt; a steaming plate of saffron rice; blackberries bleeding on the grass; the light green and yellow of pistachio kernels; hard clotted chunks of cream in a sandwich ice-cream; the collective reverence of people leaning over the tomb of a poet; the scent of orange blossoms and fear; armed men in balaclavas hiding in the attic; the roar of jet fighters; the crushed persimmons in the rubble of her neighbour's house; running away at the sight of border guards; a train whistling in the dark; a dilapidated house on the outskirts of a foreign city; a kind officer at the UN; letters, hurried phone calls, running out of telephone tokens before saying good-bye; a plane taking off; what cracks in her heart when the immigration officer shouts, "Refugees to that side"; white; cold; vast; Christmas lights; waiting for letters, for news, for a familiar voice over the phone; a quiet, half-choked sob in the middle of sleep; the language she first spoke in but no longer recognizes; home is a poem left unfinished.

Monster

by Michael Callaghan

Shortlisted, Edinburgh Flash Fiction Award 2025

There's a monster in our cellar.

I hear it scratching and moaning and muttering when I'm in bed at night. I imagine it with its yellow fangs and bloody claws and pure white eyes.
Trying to get out.
And find me.
And eat me.

Last week, I told Kevin. Kevin's my best friend. But Kevin shook his head. I was crazy, he said. There's no such thing as monsters, he said.
> But he's wrong.
> There's a monster in our cellar.

Three days ago I told Dad. He laughed. It was just the pipes making noises, he said. There's no such thing as monsters, he said.
> But he's wrong.
> There's a monster in our cellar.

Yesterday I told my teacher. She smiled. I was just having nightmares, she said. There's no such thing as monsters, she said.
> But she's wrong.
> There's a monster in our cellar.

Tonight, Dad made hotdogs for dinner. After dinner we had ice-cream and watched the news. A girl who lives nearby went missing last week and they still can't find her. After the news I went to bed. When Dad hugged me goodnight I told him to please be careful and not go in the cellar. He smiled. He would just be watching TV, he said. But later I heard the TV switch off and the sound of Dad's footsteps. I heard the cellar door creak open, then close.

I'm so scared for Dad. Nobody believes me. But they're wrong.

There's a monster in our cellar.

The Farce of Mr and Mrs Curtin

by Joe Evans

Shortlisted, Edinburgh Flash Fiction Award 2025

They married in Merton and repaired to Horton-cum-Studely for dinner and board in a country house, recently restored by a failed librettist who could barely afford to repoint the stones or have the manor re-floored, but the cracks were covered by winsome roses whose blooms were sublime and scent diverting to Mr and Mrs Burt T. Curtin.

So deeply enamoured were the pair, that finding themselves alone on the stair, they tried a door and tumbled inside for a quick amore. Now, the librettist was fretting that an elderly guest had expressed distress that the clefts in his door would enable anyone, so inclined to molest, to see him in a vulnerable state of undress. Merely as a test, the librettist crouched down at the ingress and spied Mrs Curtin pale and unfrocked; her husband, shuddering supine on the bed, shirt torn and pulled up over his head. The librettist started to cramp, fell against the door: the floor was hard; the view hardcore. At that moment the ceiling above them bowed and broke, and amid the dust and plaster of the splintered disaster, sprawled breathless and naked, two other guests – one the elderly resident of this very suite, the other a bishop, proud and effete.

In this embarrassing pink calamity, the librettist could think of nothing to restore the amity, but to offer everyone a drink. Corks were popped, Champagne guzzled, and with cheeks flushed and limbs hurting, they toasted the marriage of Mr and Mrs Burt T. Curtin.

Three Drops of Spite

by Ellen Forkin

Shortlisted, Edinburgh Flash Fiction Award 2025

I am witching and nobody knows it. I stalk the darkened streets; I'm nothing but a shadow on a wall, a rook on the wing, a wisp of curling smoke on the breeze. I slip through the open window. A whirl of dust across the floor until – up! – I'm a cat upon your bed. You sleep, slack-mouthed and unaware. You, who pointed your hairy finger at me, and cried of sickening cows. Fevered children. Rotten crops. Plague. You, who dared utter the word:

'Witch!'

This town, they believed you. I cannot buy fish at the market. I cannot walk outside without snarls and narrowing eyes and globules of spit. I cannot eat my supper in peace.

So here I am. You have summoned me. Witch by name. Witch by nature.

I sit on your chest. A heaviness. A hag. A nightmare you cannot awake from. I sit, twiddling the small bottle that holds your fate. I grin into the murk. Pop the cork. Three drops on your ale-furred tongue. Your eyes flicker, your brow beads with sweat, you dream of me but cannot move. I slink to the open window, a cat in the moonlight, thinking of my power, my skills, my witching.

Will they burn me? Probably. Will you be there? Well. I think of the belladonna berries, squishing them between finger and thumb, catching the juice in a bottle.

Sicken a cow? Never. Kill a man? Easy.

The missing half of me was last seen at an Exxon Mobil on Highway 48

by Katy Hughes

Shortlisted, Edinburgh Flash Fiction Award 2025

Car confession isn't scheduled; we'll be on the highway and one of us will turn and say "now?" Then we'll get to it, facing forward, no eye contact, offloading all the ways we've messed up.

Anything shared gets a free pass. No responding, no mentioning it later. It's how both our affairs came out, how I admitted reversing over the cat, how he told me a crypto scam had swallowed most of our savings. We've never broken the rule.

But this.

It's not that it's heinous: it isn't. Its consequences in the real world are negligible. But it changes everything. Everything I know about him, me, our life together.

And now? To break the seal of the car confessional would ruin us more than the confession. Every buried marriage misdemeanour laid out on the autopsy table again. But to carry on, without understanding how I lived every day beside this stranger? Unthinkable.

The wall between us is already impenetrable when we stop for gas; he knows as well as me there's no way back.

As he enters the store I make a split-second decision. He realises what I'll do at the same moment I realise it myself, turns in the doorway to meet my eyes. We stare. I suppose he's seeing who he always sees, but I'm looking at him for the first time. Then I put the car in gear and pull slowly out of the lot. He doesn't move, save for a slight slump of the shoulders.

The Soil Falling Over My Head

by Marianne MacRae

Shortlisted, Edinburgh Flash Fiction Award 2025

I flick through the photographs. Me dressed as a bald man with a limp; she laid on a towel in the rain pretending it's summer. Pain, just below the jugular, as though someone is trying to get out of there using a tin opener.

We were close in that obsessive, can't-live-without-you, teenaged way. Her mother called us cake mix, so enmeshed were our ingredients.

But then one evening I knocked on her door to ask if she wanted to roll eggs down the hill (a favourite hobby of ours).

'I can't,' she said. 'I've fallen into a depression. My despair will drown you.'

'I'm a good swimmer.'

'Not good enough,' she muttered. Behind her, a dinner party in full swing and an empty place just big enough for her to fill. Unbelievable. The only thing she knew how to cook was toast.

I took our friendship from around my neck and put it in a small box shaped like a mausoleum.

I handed it over. 'Bring this back if you want to talk.'

A few years later I saw the box in a charity shop. It was empty but for a few blades of grass, each one a tiny green knife. I called her on her old number.

'Hello?' she shouted over the carnival of deceit going on in the background.

'It's me.'

'It was never you,' she said, before putting the phone down like a cancer-ridden Labrador – tenderly, and not without guilt, but still, in a way, premeditated murder.

The Coal Thieves

by Frankie McMillan

Shortlisted, Edinburgh Flash Fiction Award 2025

We whistle like men as we push the wheelbarrows, and those without barrows sling a burlap sack over their shoulder and away we go hauling ourselves up the slag heap and as the soot thickens, blackens our moving shapes – *watch out*, one of us cries, wary how the slag can suddenly shift, swallow whole a woman with a barrow – while another grunts as she lifts a lump of coal closer to her eyes, places it in the wheelbarrow, as tender as any baby.

We whistle like men until our throats are clagged with soot, our necks bridled by the strain, our faces lost in the black until one of us slips as she sorts through the breakers and we scramble blindly towards her, haul her up, put her hands to the barrow, *the fire will burn tonight* we say, or don't say, but it's there in our eyes and then straight down we come from the slag heap, calling out to each other, pushing the heavy coal, the creaky wheels a lullaby of sorts.

We whistle like men when we hear the patrol, the company police who take our sacks, break our barrows, send us running, but mostly on the way home, our backs aching, our eyes streaming, the only whistling we do is the noise between our teeth, the crooning noise of old

women coming home in the dark, fondling a lump of coal
in each pocket.

Don't think of the wentletraps and scallops

by Jill Munro

Shortlisted, Edinburgh Flash Fiction Award 2025

Think of the glint and the scaly flap back and forth, her progress across pebbles from sea to kiosk. This is not a periwinkle blue and white painted booth for selling seashells – envisage instead a three-storey tall black weatherboarded building in Hastings, home to nets and buoys and fisherfolk. Imagine her slither, her ultimate waterproofing, but do not try to see a hooded aquamarine puffer jacket, black leggings, or silver highlighted hair. In fact, see no hair. Also, don't watch her rattle the anchor-shaped padlock, or rub out the word 'Closed' from the blackboard on the door.

Instead, see Ray in his blooded brown apron, as he chalks 'Open' on the board, draws a smiley face in the 'O' and adds eight curling legs. See him hairless too, bald as an octopus or, indeed, a ray. Smell salt air, a linger of fishy aroma. See him write up the catch of the day – Dover Sole, Plaice, Mackerel, Brill and double-cross his pound signs per kilo. Think of the clear blue June sky, the scud of the clouds, picture the whiteness of the spume.

Visualise Ray stroking his hand across the cold, wet, silken flat of her skin, feeling the shiver as he lays her on ice, checks for no final twitch, watches her glassy, left-eyed stare, as he tenderly begins the filleting for a customer, declares her the best brill of this morning's catch. 'She's better than any turbot, my love, smaller flakes, a sweeter taste.'

The Punishment

by Laurie Swinarton

Shortlisted, Edinburgh Flash Fiction Award 2025

Dóchas' mother scurries along the dusty path, yanking the little girl. Dóchas is nearly aloft, a kite buffeted by rough winds.

Dóchas cries, prays. She envisions herself going topsy-turvy over the cliff, smashing against rocks, limbs whirling in the sea like laundry on washday. She imagines water monsters tightening 'round her, hugging her into stillness.

But she thinks of the shed and knows *anything* else is better.

She slides through blackish sheep shit, stumbles, stalls. Sour, slurred words wriggle from her mother's mouth: 'Tá tú leisciúil. Horrid child!'

Her mother's red hands press warnings into her fingers. Her mother's hands, so changeable. Yesterday they popped figs into Dóchas' mouth, braided her hair. But today? Unreasonable, full of spite.

Dóchas weaves a skin of alertness. But always her mother deftly cuts through it.

Now her mother shoves her into the hut. A pinch of light cuts through a slat of wood and illuminates the scene. Apples, bread, water. A bench for sitting, waiting.

The door slams, her heart screams.

'Please?' Dóchas asks, not for the first time. Her tiny fingers brush against the door lock. She senses her mother, restless, on the other side.

Her mother lumbers away and Dóchas knows she'll be back in four, five, six days. With gentle hands, sweet breath.

She counts apples, hunkers down. Jagged feelings bubble up behind her breastbone. She tries to climb into herself.

Dóchas wants to be good but will likely turn into a wild thing as hours, minutes, seconds creep away.

Undignified Dignity

by Ruth Thomason

Shortlisted, Edinburgh Flash Fiction Award 2025

I did not shy away when I was called... we knew a time
would come when... well... the phrase "personal care"
covers it. You, an old lady, powerless leg daubed in
orange... my mother... needing a shower after the
butchery of joints. Me, a slightly less old lady... strength
still in my limbs. Yes I will help you... yes I will wash
you... it is just skin and bodies... we will not be
embarrassed. We will not.

And here we were at the precipice we knew awaited us...
onward... and your nightie was off, the walker aimed
toward the en suite. Our eyes either avert lest anything be
seen... or we look directly at each other... in the eyes...
do not crumble with pity or shame... the moment for
dignity is here... I am your hook to hang your dignity
upon... I hold your dignity high... chin up... the walker,
the walkee and the walked shuffled on.

The shower cubicle is narrow... I had to pull you in
towards me because there was a step up... there was no
other way.

And now... idiots that we are... we are wedged in. Me
wedged against the back corner... your powerless body
blocking me... with no way to step back. We two women
laughed... howled at our predicament... "We might die

here!!" we snorted... your skin and familiar smell pressed against me.

I wriggled out, mum. I helped you.

All that it entails

by Jody Timmerman

Shortlisted, Edinburgh Flash Fiction Award 2025

Emma gazed out the window as she waited for the P.E.T. meeting to begin. The winter had been so warm that Jack Frost was forced to go on the dole. She smiled at her musings. Emma loved the cold weather as it necessitated layers of clothing. She felt safe. Why her parents had not opted for a noninvasive corrective procedure at her birth remained a mystery. No doubt they did not want to interfere with God's plan but surely God did not want her to suffer the unbearable humiliation. Now as an adult she had become strangely attached to that which made her unique and more real rather than less human. Affliction or enhancement? That was the unanswerable question. Her body's outward show of her pleasure no longer filled her with embarrassment. She felt fortunate to find this newly formed support group of people who were configured like her and felt proud of their extra appendage. Emma was awakened from her reverie by the moderator's opening "Welcome to the second annual meeting of People Exhibiting Tails."

Edinburgh True Flash Award 2025

First Prize
Sophie Olszowski, *All That Time*

Highly Commended
Beverley Casebow, *On The Road*
Stephanie Taylor, *Mermaid*

Editor's Choice
Peter Stewart, *A Curious Incident*

All that time

by Sophie Olszowski

Winner, Edinburgh True Flash Award 2025

After he died, she studied books about stages of grief, keeping a watchful eye to see if she was getting them right, but thought it unlikely: when she'd lost her mother, an article asserted 'The bereaved jump when the phone rings' yet then, as now, she sat stock still as calls went unanswered, so she supposed she wasn't a very compliant griever.

She read hungrily, searching for him, clutching onto poems that understood her, to experts who relented about their cherished stages, admitting they're not linear, that some days are like the first.

As years passed, solitude became both what she craved and a lacuna into which she feared she might slip and drown. She wondered how he'd have fared if she'd died first, comforted that he hadn't had to do these hard yards while guessing he'd have made quicker work of them; he'd been so good at life.

Once he'd said to her, perhaps recognising the likelihood of just this time, 'You do know we'll always have each other?' And she hadn't really understood, but assumed he, the deep, lapsed, Catholic, had insider knowledge, knew there'd be a reunion of some kind, while she (the uninitiated agnostic) could only wonder how it might look, where it might happen.

Until one day, she saw there had been no spaces; while she'd been wondering why go on living, he'd been with her at every breath, in every molecule. Just as he'd promised, he'd been everywhere, all that time.

On The Road

by Beverley Casebow

Highly Commended. Edinburgh True Flash Award 2025

He arrived one morning with two carrier bags and set up camp at the end of the street. By lunchtime there was a bike, a Primus stove, a tarpaulin, a radio, and numerous bin bags of belongings filling the small triangle of waste land.

He never asked for money, but when I passed a few days later, he told me about a heart problem, and a constant cough. 'I need vitamin C', he said. I offered him the blueberries that I'd just bought. He shook his head. 'It's cranberries I want. And some Ginkgo biloba. Also sugar-free jam from the Polish supermarket if you're passing.' He knew the herbs for every ailment.

The next day he asked for music. 'Could you download some John Barry?' he asked, handing me a memory stick. 'That's what I long for most.' At night, I could hear Radio 3 on the breeze.

On the third morning, he seemed agitated. 'They're after me,' he said. I looked for the police, but saw only two crows, bobbing and cawing on the brick wall.

After seven days the wind got up. His silver foil blanket was swept up and away, spiralling over the roof of the old folk's home. 'A sign,' he said, 'to be moving on. The wind knows best when it's time to go.'

When I came home from work that day, he was gone. His patch of ground empty, like he'd never been. There was only a solitary black crow picking for worms.

Mermaid

by Stephanie Taylor

Highly Commended, Edinburgh True Flash Award 2025

One time I breathed under water because I knew I had mermaid blood flowing in my veins.

It was at school swimming lessons.

As everyone else splashed and coughed on the surface thrashing to the other side, I glided beneath them, my fingers trailing over the grainy tiles with the rough grout dips between. I looked up to the foaming chaos of arms and legs above. Shards of sun from the roof lights split through the water atoms and lit up the pool, surrounding me in their brilliance. I was so calm.

Breathe, they said and I did.

The water was like warm silk as it filled my lungs as natural as hot cocoa on a winter's day by my granny's hissing gas fire. I watched as the frenetic flailing continued just out of my reach. They were so near yet so very far.

I was cocooned in my otherness.

The serenity was exhilarating. I had known it all along and it was true. I vowed to keep it to myself. All your biggest, best thoughts get small when you hear what people say about them.

But I couldn't help it.

In the changing rooms all boiling trying to force spaghetti damp limbs into school shirts and tights, it just spilled out.

I breathed underwater just then, I said, and everyone went quiet.

Helen looked at me as if I was a disgusting absurd thing and said,

Well obviously, anyone can do that.

A Curious Incident

by Peter Stewart

Editor's Choice, Shortlisted, Edinburgh True Flash Award 2025

When my mum took a course in autism, she decided my dad was autistic. She declared my uncle autistic, her sister-in-law autistic, that whole side of the clan autistic. When my dad heard the characteristics of autism he said, 'That sounds like Peter. Peter is the autistic one.'

Personally, I think mum's interest in autism and the signs of autism and the cataloguing of her relatives into degrees of autism is itself pretty autistic.

But one time I was at a party and noticed an Omagh lad watching me. He stood at the edge of the group and just seemed a watchful character. At one point, I made a joke about me being on the spectrum. The man from Omagh frowned.

'Peter,' he said. 'Are you autistic?'

I tried to laugh it off. 'I don't know,' I laughed. 'I could be.'

'Because I've noticed you've got all the symptoms.'

'What symptoms?' I asked, less cheerfully.

Then the lad from Omagh made a speech. You know that scene in a murder mystery when the detective corners his suspects and starts laying out all the clues and this speech is so exhaustive in its detail, so relentless in its logic, so evocative in its imagery that the murderer is left reeling and has no choice but to confess? This speech was like that speech.

'Right,' I said when he was finished.

I don't know why that boy had been observing me so closely all evening. I suspect he was probably autistic.

Human, Probably

by James Aitcheson

Shortlisted, Edinburgh True Flash Award 2025

Rita is planting potatoes with her grandmother when she sees the monster. Bright orange, the size of a person. Its head is huge and white. It lumbers across the furrowed field. It's coming this way.

The secret is not to plant them too close together, her grandmother says. Are you listening?

Rita tugs at her grandmother's sleeve, saying, Look!

The monster, closer now, takes off its head. No, not its head. A helmet. Holding the helmet under its arm, it calls out a greeting. It sounds like a man. Speaking Russian. That means he's human, probably.

Straightaway her grandmother shouts back, demanding to know who he is, where he's from, how he got here. He replies that he came on a ship, but that's impossible. There's no sea anywhere near here.

I came from the sky, he says. Don't be afraid. I am a Soviet citizen, like you. Do you have a telephone? I must call Moscow.

On his helmet, in red letters: CCCP. Rita's too young to be able to read properly, but she understands what these letters mean. He's a friend.

I have returned from orbiting the Earth in my capsule, he says, grinning. The first man in space! What do you think of that, little one?

Rita doesn't know what she thinks. What is space? What is orbiting? What is capsule? But she knows that she likes this wide-eyed young man, with his big ears and his big smile.

I am Yuri, he says. What's your name?

Almost

by Bridget Goldschmidt

Shortlisted, Edinburgh True Flash Award 2025

We were standing on the corner, talking. I asked whether he had plans for the upcoming three-day weekend.

'It's such a hassle to get into the city,' he said, shrugging, as though it were on the other side of the earth, and not a mere 25-minute ferry ride away. 'You?'

'I might see a movie,' I answered, adding, to prolong the conversation, 'I guess you'll stay home?'

'Yup. Maybe hang out with friends.'

There was nothing more to say, yet we stood there as though the scene had ended but the director hadn't yelled 'cut,' so the camera was still rolling.

'If this were a movie,' I thought, 'this would be when we lean in and kiss.' I started to lean. He seemed to lean, too.

Then a taxi's horn blared and we both drew back, ourselves again.

'I'd better go,' he said, the first to make a move. 'Have a good one,' he added, rushing past me to catch his bus to the ferry. 'See you Tuesday.'

'See you,' I echoed, although he was already halfway down the street. 'If it were ever going to happen,' I thought, 'that would have been the moment.'

But if it hadn't been a taxi's horn, it would have been a rustle of pigeon wings, or someone shouting into a cell phone, or nothing at all. For two such captive souls as ours, timing was everything in making a break for it, and we had missed our time.

Morning on Merrion Square

by Liz Houchin

Shortlisted, Edinburgh True Flash Award 2025

My thoughts grasp at spears of sunlight but are dragged under a riptide of meds and sleep.

I remember only the cold man voice contoured to hide his boredom with this tiresome woman and all the tiresome women. *'Let's get Mum down to theatre, baby is getting a little tired,'* he says. A little close to organ failure, he means. And then sleep.

And now it's morning on Merrion Square. Dark red flashes and flares tell me that I am awake and so I must be alive. But what kind of alive? Because an alive mother with a dead baby is a different kind of alive.

The nurses are laughing too far away to see my ears pool with terror and unknowing. Maybe I don't want to know. Because the big question is bigger than girl or boy or big or small. But it's time to leave this in-between space. There's a new voice at the end of the bed saying *'Hey'* in his whisper voice which isn't really ever a whisper. But I don't mind that now. If he is here, I am not alone. I hadn't thought of him until this moment, something I will keep to myself. He was helpless too in the fluorescent fog. It's time for me to know what he knows.

My eyes meet his smile. He holds a blue blanket with a baby inside. And he says everything's fine and he hopes I don't mind that he gave him the name Benjamin.

It's been raining all morning and the playground is treacherous

by Heather Norton

Shortlisted, Edinburgh True Flash Award 2025

Indoors, my second-grade teacher forbids us to venture near the merry-go-round. She warns us off with tales of the big kids. How they'll spin it too fast. How they'll cause us to fall. She looks directly at me, and I return her pointed stare, impatience bubbling up inside. It's too late for caution. Vivid images of the swamp-like moat now encircling its edges have taken hold.

The bell rings.

I dash across the field, thin canvas shoes taking on water with every squish. I'm not on long before an older boy asks if I want to go faster. I say yes because I've never wanted anything more. He stretches his lanky body out, bridging himself across the murky divide. Dirty, white sneakers beat a blurry path just beyond the water's edge. I can't hold on for more than a few seconds. It feels like forever.

I am sent to the principal's office once my teacher runs out of breath. My mother is called, humiliated again. She will be furious. Stomach churning as the violent drive home plays out in my mind, I change into a sweatshirt and sweatpants with the school logo embroidered on each. I bury my nose in the soft, floral scent. My own clothes never smell like this.

Told to wait on a bench, I sense a familiar exhaustion around me – with me – but I'd been happy for one brief moment, heart pounding as I hung on with all my might.

Leftovers

by Mandy Wheeler

Shortlisted, Edinburgh True Flash Award 2025

You sit in silence with the nurse, the plastic Ziplock bag between you.

Finally, you say: 'Really? A Ziplock bag? The kind of thing you use for leftovers in the fridge. You think that's appropriate?'

The nurse shrugs.

'This is everything your mother had with her when she was admitted.'

'You couldn't stretch to paper? Or cloth. A cloth bag – now that would have been nice. That would have offered a bit of privacy. Don't we all deserve that at the end? The opportunity to conceal, a last chance to tease? If it were cloth, there could be anything in there. There could be a gun in there.'

The nurse rolls her eyes and indicates a sheet of paper.

'Check the contents and sign for receipt.'

You read the list: *A silver St Christopher keychain, a British Heart Foundation badge, a bus pass, a red plastic purse with gold clasp (cracked).*

At 'cracked' you look up. 'Excuse me, but why...?'

The nurse shrugs and looks away.

A throat lozenge, some tissues, a mint.

'And that's it? No diary or love letters? No cinema tickets, scribbled phone numbers, restaurant bills, dry-cleaning receipts? A fake passport? Some photographs?'

'No photographs.'

'So, she could be anybody?'

'I guess.'

That night the nurse feels bad about the eye rolling. She wonders if she's burnt out as she finds she can remember almost nothing of the woman who sat opposite her today. Just another disappointed daughter picking through the debris, searching for clues.

Printed in Dunstable, United Kingdom

72925939R00143